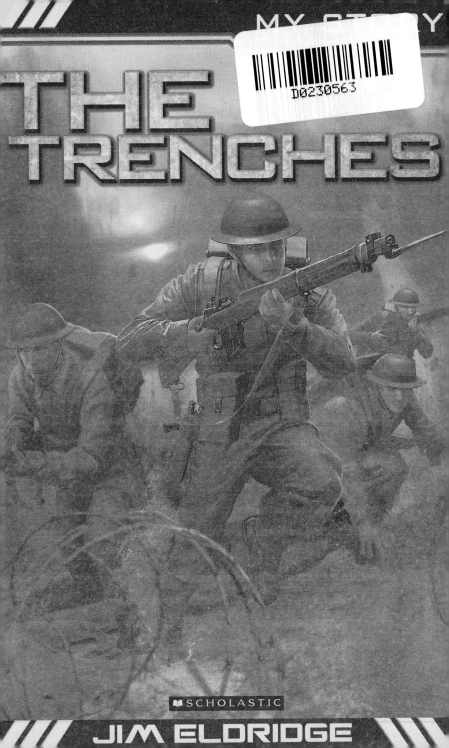

To my wife, Lynne

While the events described and some of the characters in this book may be based on actual historical events and real people, Billy Stevens is a fictional character, created by the author, and his story is a work of fiction.

Scholastic Children's Books
Euston House, 24 Eversholt Street,
London, NW1 1DB, UK
A division of Scholastic Ltd
London ~ New York ~ Toronto ~ Sydney ~ Auckland
Mexico City ~ New Delhi ~ Hong Kong

First published in the UK by Scholastic Ltd, 2002
This edition published by Scholastic Ltd, 2014

Text copyright © Jim Eldridge, 2002

ISBN 978 1407 13673 8

Typeset by M Rules
Printed and bound by CPI Group (UK) Ltd, Croydon, CR0 4YY

2 4 6 8 10 9 7 5 3 1

The right of Jim Eldridge to be identified as the author of this work has been asserted by him in accordance with the Copyright, Designs and Patents Act, 1988.

# CARLISLE, 1919

It all began just five years ago, but in those five years everything has changed. In that time I've lost good friends, and made new ones. I've changed from Billy Stevens, the innocent boy from Carlisle, to Billy Stevens, a man whose mind is still filled with memories of terrible sights that I hope no one else has to see or live through. This is my story, told while those memories are still vivid in my mind. But I don't think they'll ever go away…

## 1914

My family – that is, me, my parents, my two brothers and two sisters – lived in a part of Carlisle called Denton Holme. It was all red-brick terraced houses and cramped cobbled streets. Other parts of Carlisle were richer, with bigger houses, but I liked where we lived. It was friendly. In Denton everyone knew everyone else, and you'd always find someone to help you out if you were in trouble, or short of money for milk, or coal or anything.

Rob Matthews and I had been best mates since we started at school together. I suppose we became best pals because we were sat together when we were first in Miss Pursley's class and we used to walk home together because our houses were round the corner from each other. But there's more to it than that. You don't stay best pals with someone just because you live near them.

Rob was always the dare-devil of the two of us, the one leading the way. He was the one who climbed the highest up the trees to get the pick of the crop when we scrumped apples from Mrs Gardner's orchard. Me, I was content to pick up windfalls from the ground. And Rob wasn't afraid to tell our bullying teacher, Mr Dickens, what he thought of him when Dickens picked on some poor innocent kid in our class. It got Rob a beating from Dickens with the cane, but Rob just took it and didn't let him see that it hurt him.

Like I say, that was Rob Matthews. He was a hero to the boys – and the girls – at school and around Denton, and he was my best pal. What he saw in me, I don't know. Although he said once, "You're clever with your head. I like that."

Rob and I were both thirteen years old when the War broke out. There'd been talk about it coming for some time, though I hadn't paid much interest before because it was all just politics as far as I was concerned, and politicians talking was just boring. But I had picked up things from listening to my dad when he'd sit and read the paper and talk about what was going on about the Kaiser – who was the Emperor of Germany – with my Uncle Stanley when he came round.

I remember sitting in our tiny kitchen cooking potatoes in their skins in the range, while my dad and Uncle Stanley shared the newspaper, and Dad read out from his bit, the sports pages, and Uncle Stanley read bits out from the pages that had the news.

"There's a horse racing at Epsom today called Stevens Luck," said Dad, rustling his paper. "I wonder if it's worth a shilling each way?"

That was the way it was with my dad: he'd check the horses and spend all day thinking about whether to put a bet on or not. I had no doubt that if he'd had spare money he would have, but in our house money was so tight that he never did. This was lucky, because most of the horses he mentioned as likely winners never came anywhere.

The front page of the section that Uncle Stanley held said "WAR DECLARED" in big letters. "It had to come," sighed Uncle Stanley. "I could tell it was coming when they killed Franz Ferdinand."

"Who's Franz Ferdinand?" I asked.

"He was the Archduke Franz Ferdinand of Austria," Uncle Stanley told me. "Him and his wife were on a visit to Serbia and they got killed by a bunch of lunatics. Anarchists."

"Why?" I asked.

"Politics," said my dad. "Believe me, son, politics is to blame for most of the troubles in this world."

"As soon as that happened, I knew we were in for trouble," Uncle Stanley continued. That was the way with Uncle Stanley. Once something major had happened he could tell you how he always knew that it was going to happen. However, just like with Dad's racing forecasts, Uncle Stanley never seemed to be able to tell us what was going to happen *before* it did.

"Once Franz Ferdinand was killed there was only one thing that was bound to happen: Austria and Hungary declared war on Serbia. It was obvious."

"Why?" I asked.

Uncle Stanley ignored my question, and carried on: "Of course, straight away Russia declared its support for Serbia."

"There's another horse here called Archduke," muttered Dad, still studying the racing form. "It's 100-1. Now that's what I call good odds."

Uncle Stanley glared at my dad, slightly annoyed because he wasn't paying attention to all this knowledge unfolding, but my dad just ignored him. He was used to Uncle Stanley.

"Why did Russia get involved?" I asked. "And why are we at war?"

"Alliances," said my dad, still concentrating on his racing page. "Countries sign agreements to back each other up in case they're attacked."

"Exactly," nodded Uncle Stanley. "In this case, Germany, who are on Austria and Hungary's side, told Russia to stay out of it. Russia refused, so Germany declared war on Russia. Then straight away Germany set out to invade France."

"Which had been the Germans' plan all along, if you ask me," said Dad.

"Exactly," nodded Uncle Stanley again. "That's what I've always said. It's obvious. But to do that the Germans have got to go through Belgium. And Britain has got a treaty with Belgium, so that if Belgium were ever attacked we would come to its defence. So, when Germany invaded Belgium, we had no choice but to declare war on Germany." Uncle Stanley prodded the headline on the paper with his finger.

"And that, Billy, is how this war started." He gave a smile, pleased at having imparted his knowledge of world politics to me. "Mind," he added, "it'll all be over by Christmas. The Germans can't fight a war against proper soldiers like ours. I know what I'm talking about…"

As you can imagine, as soon as we knew that war had been declared, me and Rob and all the boys in our street all went down to the army recruiting office to join up and fight the Hun. But the Sergeant there just laughed and told us all to go away.

"Don't you worry," he said. "It'll all be over in a few weeks. We'll soon kick the Kaiser back to Germany."

I was really disappointed. All the way down to the Recruiting Office I'd had visions of myself in my khaki uniform and my tin helmet rushing forward in battle, firing my rifle, and taking loads of Germans prisoners and getting medals. I could even see myself at Buckingham Palace getting my medal for bravery from the King. Instead of fighting bravely we were being sent home and we'd all still have to go to school tomorrow.

Rob was even angrier than I was. "It's not fair," he said. "When there's a war on they ought to take everyone who wants to go. It makes sense that the more soldiers we've got on our side the bigger our army will be and the quicker we'll win."

"Maybe the Germans'll be harder to beat than the Sergeant thinks," I suggested. "Maybe it'll go on for longer and then they'll want us soon enough."

"Maybe," said Rob. "We can but hope."

Well, the Kaiser didn't get kicked back to Germany in a few weeks. In fact the weeks turned into months, and then the months turned into years, and all those people who'd been so confident it would all be over in a short space of time were now moaning and groaning about the country going to ruin because of the War.

My Grandfather Pickles, my dad's father, told me, "It wouldn't be going on this long if the old Queen, Victoria, were still alive. She'd have put a stop to it. She'd just have a word with her nephew, Kaiser Billy, and tell him to pack up his soldiers and go back home."

I must admit, I was surprised to find out that our king and the German kaiser were cousins. But when I told Rob this he just laughed and said didn't I know how families were always fighting among themselves. Like his mother and her sister, who were always arguing hammer and tongs.

As the War dragged on, Rob and I often talked about joining up and going out and fighting. We saw ourselves as the heroes who would go over to Belgium and France and sort those Germans out. Both of us were really eager to get out there, but there was one problem: our mums.

When my mum found out that I'd been down to the Recruiting Office soon after the War started, she was furious. "Don't you even think about joining up!" she said. "If you go over to France I'll never see you again!"

"Course you will," I said. "I'll be allowed home on leave."

"That's not what I mean and you know it!" she said angrily. "You're not going and that's that! So don't you even think about it!"

After a few months, I brought the matter up again, but Mum hadn't changed her mind about it one bit.

"You're not going!" she said when I mentioned I was thinking of joining up.

"He's only thinking of defending his country!" my dad put in, defending me.

"Oh yes," snapped back my mum. "And he'll come home with bits missing, like Brian Cotterill over in Botchergate. Twenty years old, and no legs now. What chance has Brian Cotterill got of ever earning a decent living?"

"They don't all come home injured," said my dad.

"No, some come home dead," snapped my mum. "And some don't come home at all."

With that she gathered up the bundle of washing she'd been packing in a sheet and went next door to use Mrs Higsons's copper washer.

Dad looked at me and sighed. "Your mum's got very

strong opinions," he said. "That's because she lost an uncle in the Boer War. She doesn't really mean it."

But I knew she did, and it made me feel miserable. I wanted to be out there, fighting for my king and country. Instead I was stuck at home while other boys from Carlisle went off and became heroes.

At the start of 1917, the year I turned sixteen, the War had been going on for over two years. I'd been working as a trainee telegraph operator at the Citadel Railway Station in Carlisle for two years, ever since I left school. Being a telegraph operator meant sitting at a desk and operating a telegraph key. This key sent messages along cables to the other railway stations along the lines. It also received them, printing the messages out in Morse code, a series of short buzzes and long buzzes, each one representing a letter, so the telegraph operator had to be able to understand the code to be able to read and send messages.

Rob had also got a job on the railway. He didn't work on the telegraph, though, he worked as a track layer, laying railway lines. He was a big tough lad, was Rob, and he could wield a hammer and drive a spike as good as men twice his age.

By January 1917, stories were coming back from Belgium about how our troops only needed one last push and they'd break the Germans, but the Germans had dug in tight. If only more troops could be got out there to the Front, which was where the fighting was going on, the Germans would crack and the war would be over. More men were all that was needed. I was getting more and more eager to get out there, and so was Rob.

"We have to go!" he said to me one day as we walked home from work. "I can't stand just hanging around reading about the War in the papers. I want to be out there, winning it!"

But Rob's mum felt as strongly about him not going as mine did. And so we stayed in Carlisle, getting more and more frustrated.

Around February time, posters started being put up on walls around Carlisle and leaflets put through letter boxes, all saying the same thing: "Are You A Man or A Mouse?" They were put out by Lord Lonsdale, the local lord, who had set up his own regiment for local men soon after the War started.

I read one of the posters. It said:

*Are You A Man or A Mouse? Are you a man who will forever be handed down to posterity as a Gallant Patriot? Or are you to be handed down to posterity as a ROTTER and a COWARD? If you are a Man, NOW is your opportunity of proving it. Enlist at once and go to the nearest Recruiting Officer."*

Rob had also seen the poster. "They're calling us cowards now," he said angrily.

I knew how he felt. Sometimes I felt ashamed, walking to work, and knowing that other boys of my age were already out in Belgium fighting to defend us. Some women had been seen giving out white feathers to young men who they felt should have been out fighting on the Front. I dreaded the moment when a woman might come up and give me a white feather in the street in front of everyone.

After seeing the poster, I brooded all day at work on the whole business of going off to war. Rob must have been doing the same, because as we met up after work, Rob said suddenly: "Do you still want to join up?"

"Of course I do," I said.

"Then let's go and do it."

I frowned.

"What's the problem?" Rob asked. "We both want to go out there and do our bit, stop the Hun. Lord Lonsdale wants people like us."

"My mum won't like it," I said doubtfully. "Nor will yours."

Rob laughed. "Then we won't tell them till we've done it," he said. "Once we're in, they won't be able to say anything about it. And I bet you that secretly your mum will be pleased to have a soldier in the family."

I thought about it and hoped Rob was right. Maybe once I'd joined, Mum would accept it. She wouldn't have a choice.

"Right," I agreed determinedly. "Let's do it."

So that very afternoon, instead of going straight home, we went to the Recruiting Office the Lonsdale Battalion had set up in the town centre. A Recruiting Sergeant was standing guard at the door, looking very smart and straight, his boots shining, his uniform smelling of starch.

"Yes, young men," he boomed. "What can I do for you?"

"We've come to join up," said Rob.

"Good!" beamed the Recruiting Sergeant. "How old are you?"

"Sixteen," said Rob.

The Sergeant looked at Rob and said, "Sorry, son, you're too young. Come back when you're nineteen." Then he gave Rob a wink and said, "Tomorrow, eh?"

Next he turned to me and said, "And what about you?"

"I'm nineteen," I said, thinking quickly.

"Good," smiled the Sergeant. "Come on in. Your country needs you."

Rob looked at me, his mouth open. For the first time in our lives I had beaten him to something. Then his face broke into a grin and he said: "I'll see you tomorrow, Billy. When I'm nineteen."

With that, he gave me a wink, and then hurried home.

"Don't tell your mum!" I called after him. "She might tell mine and I want to tell her myself!"

"Don't worry," he called back. "I won't."

When I got home, Mum was looking worried.

"Where have you been?" she demanded. "Your supper's been in the oven this whole hour, waiting for you."

"I joined up in the army," I said. "I'm going to fight in the War."

Mum looked at me, shocked, and her mouth dropped open. Then she almost fell backwards on to one of the kitchen chairs so hard I thought she'd break it. Then she began to cry.

At that moment my dad came home from work. "What's up?" he asked.

"I've joined up," I said. "I've joined the Lonsdale Battalion. I start my training the day after tomorrow."

Dad gave me a big smile. I could tell he was proud of me. "Well done, son!" he said.

"No! You can't go!" sobbed my mum. "Harry, tell him he can't go! He's too young! He can't join up! He's under age!"

"I wasn't the only one who was under age," I protested. "About half of the recruits who were in the Recruiting Office were under nineteen. In fact they let William Chambers join up, and he's only thirteen."

"That's criminal!" said my mum angrily, and she burst into tears again.

"There, there," said my dad, and he went to her and put his arm around her to cuddle her. He then gave me a wink and a nod of his head to say, "Leave this to me, son. I'll take it from here."

I went out and round the corner to Rob's house and told him what had happened.

"Your mum'll get over it," he assured me. "When do you start your training?"

"Day after tomorrow," I said. "I've got tomorrow to tell them at the Citadel Station what I'm going to do, and get packed."

"Well don't go off to France without me," said Rob. "You may have joined up first, but I'm going to be there with you, and I bet when we're there I get more Huns than you do."

I don't know what Dad said to Mum, but although it didn't make her change her mind, it quietened her down. Or maybe it was just that she accepted my going. She still sniffled a lot and wiped her eyes whenever she saw me the next day, but on the whole it wasn't as bad as I thought it would be.

My brothers and sisters thought my going off to war was very exciting, and John asked me if I'd bring him back a Hun helmet as a souvenir. I promised him I'd do my best.

Rob enlisted the next day, claiming to be nineteen, and persuaded the Recruiting Sergeant that he and I needed to start our training together because we were best friends. Because the army was keen to get friends to join up together, they agreed. I had to smile at this. It was typical of Rob, being able to talk the army into letting him start training a day earlier. Anything, rather than miss out and let me be ahead of the game.

On 15 March, Rob and I began our training at Blackhall Camp, which had been set up on the racecourse just outside Carlisle. We were given uniforms of a rough, grey material with the Lonsdale's very own badge and shoulder flashes sewn on the sleeves. We were billeted in long wooden huts, with bunk-beds running along the two long walls. Rob grabbed the bottom bunk of our pair and I took the one on top.

The huts were pretty basic, just light, timber buildings, but considering they'd been put up quickly, they weren't too bad. The only thing really wrong with them was that they were cold. The walls seemed strong, but when the wind blew at night when we were asleep, it came in through the timber sheets and caused a terrible draught.

During the day we did our marching drill using wooden poles instead of rifles because we were told the soldiers at the Front needed all the rifles.

At the end of the first day, Rob looked at his pole and sniffed scornfully and said, "I hope I get a chance to practise with a real rifle before I go into battle. I don't think a wooden pole will be much use against the Hun."

We dug trenches and then filled them in again for three days on the trot. By the end of those three days my back and arms were killing me! It seemed so stupid to me, digging a trench just to fill it in again. One of the boys in our hut, Jed Lowe, said we had to learn how to dig trenches because that's what we'd be living in when we got to the Front. He reckoned he knew because his older brother was already out there in Flanders. He said we needed to fill the trenches in again so that the next lot of recruits would have somewhere to dig up, otherwise they wouldn't be able to practise digging. I supposed Jed knew what he was talking about, having a brother at the Front, but it still seemed a big waste of effort to me. To my mind, we should have been spending our energy fighting the Hun.

The weeks passed. We dug trenches. We filled them in again. We drilled. We marched. We drilled some more. I became an expert in handling a wooden pole and pretending it was a rifle.

It was in the middle of the third week that I was sent for by our Commanding Officer. I was puzzled, as was Rob. What had I done wrong that I was being summoned in this way?

An awful thought struck me. Had my mum gone to the authorities and complained about them taking me when I was under age? Was that what it was?

I put this to Rob, and he frowned and said it was possible.

"The only way to find out is to go and see what he wants," he said. That was the way with Rob. Straightforward.

Knowing he was right, but with a sinking feeling in my chest, I went to the Commanding Officer's Quarters.

Our Commanding Officer, Brigadier Reynolds, motioned me to stand at ease after I had saluted.

"Private Stevens," he said. "I understand that you worked as a trainee telegraph operator at the Citadel Railway Station in Carlisle. Is that correct?"

I was surprised by the question. I couldn't see what it had to do with my being in the army and going to fight the Huns.

"Yes, sir!" I replied.

"In that case, it looks like we'll be losing you," he said.

I was shocked. Did that mean I was going to be thrown out of the army? I knew that some people had what they called "reserve occupation" jobs, which meant the authorities felt it was more important that that person stayed in England to do that job rather than go and fight, but I couldn't see that a trainee telegraph operator came under that heading. How could they be losing me?

"But I want to go to France, sir!" I blurted out.

"Oh, you'll be going to France all right," said the Brigadier. "Only not with the Lonsdale Battalion. The Engineers are desperate for men with technical experience, especially in telegraphs and communications. So, you're being assigned to the Royal Engineers, Signals."

For the first time since we were tiny nippers, Rob and I were split up. It was strange to be saying goodbye to him. We'd been together as best mates all our lives, living in the same area, in the same classes at school, and even working at the same place, the railway station.

"Don't worry," grinned Rob as I packed my stuff up that evening, ready to go. "We'll meet up again on the Front. While I'm shooting Huns and winning medals and you're mending bits of broken wire."

I forced a grin back at this, but I had to admit that what he said rankled with me. I'd joined up to fight, not to work a telegraph key, or repair signalling equipment. I could have stayed behind in Carlisle and done that.

"Huh! Don't *you* worry," I responded. "Once I get over there I won't just be stuck working on the telegraph. As soon as the officers see how brave I am under fire I expect they'll put me up at the Front as well. I'll be shooting as many Huns as you, you can count on it."

"I'll have a head start on you," said Rob. "We're off the week after next."

I thought of what lay before me then. More training. More things to learn. Meanwhile, Rob would be out there at the Front, getting all the glory.

My face must have showed how miserable I felt about it, because Rob laughed and slapped me on the back.

"Don't put on such a long face, Billy," he grinned. "I didn't really mean it about getting more Hun than you. Come on, cheer up. We're all in the War together."

"Yes, but you'll be actually *in* the War," I said gloomily. "Me, I'll be on the edges, sending messages, just like you said."

Next morning I went off to a camp in Yorkshire for further training to be an Engineer, while Rob carried on at Blackhall Camp.

If I thought Engineer training would be easier, I was wrong. It still meant lots of digging trenches and filling them in again, just the same as before. The difference was I had extra stuff to learn.

I already knew quite a bit about Morse code and telegraph keys from my work at the Citadel Station, plus a bit about wireless. Now I had to go to lessons to learn even more. Most of it was practical stuff, how to repair a cable, fitting connections, that sort of thing.

Most of the other blokes were like me, they'd joined up to fight and found themselves put into the Engineers because of the work they did in civilian life.

One of my new pals was a fellow called Charlie Morgan. He was from Newcastle. He worked at the railway as a telegraph operator, but, being 21, he wasn't a trainee any more but a fully trained-up operator.

I liked Charlie because he was so confident about everything. He was sure we were going to win the War. He was sure he was going to be rich one day. He was going to have one of the biggest houses in Newcastle. All it took was time. It was good to have someone like Charlie as a mate, it sort of took the edge off Rob not being around any more to keep things cheerful.

I spent four weeks at the Engineers Training Camp, by the end of which I could mend a telegraph cable, and dig a ditch (and fill it in again) in my sleep. During the training, six of us Engineers had palled up. As well as me and Charlie there was Ginger Smith, Wally Clarke, Danny MacDonald and Alf Tupper. Danny was just a year older than me at eighteen, Ginger was nineteen, Charlie, Wally and Alf were in their early twenties. We'd all been working on the telegraph, which gave us something in common. Plus, we'd all volunteered to go out and fight the Hun, but had all ended up in the Engineers learning how to repair telegraph and telephone cables instead, which had annoyed all of us. But, as we'd all learned during our training, orders are orders and you didn't argue. As one of our sergeants had told us during training, "When I say 'Jump!' you don't even ask how high – you just jump! You're not in the army to ask questions!"

I knew that by now Rob and the rest of the Lonsdale Battalion would have been in France for some time, and I wondered how he was. Had he managed to bag his first Hun?

At the end of the four weeks, we were told that our training was over and at long last we were headed for the Front. I almost cheered when we got our sailing orders. At last, I was going to War!

For someone like me who'd never travelled much farther from Carlisle than the coast at Silloth, a distance of about 30 miles (unless you counted the journey from Carlisle to the Signals Unit in Yorkshire), the journey to Belgium was a really big adventure.

Charlie put on the air that this journey was nothing to him. "I've been all over the place," he told me. "Wales. Scotland. Cornwall. I've been everywhere."

"London?" asked Ginger.

"Loads of times," shrugged Charlie. "London's nothing but another Newcastle, only maybe a bit bigger."

We took a train south to London, and then another train from London to Folkestone. There we were loaded on to a troopship, which took us across the Channel from Folkestone to Boulogne. I didn't think the sea was too bad, although it was rough enough for Charlie and Alf to get seasick. At first Charlie tried to pretend that he was a seasoned traveller and it wasn't seasickness, it must have been something he ate, but when other men got seasick as well he stopped pretending.

During this long journey there was a sense of excitement among all of us. Not only were we going abroad, we were going to fight the Hun!

The train from Boulogne took us to a town called St Omer. All the way along on the train I kept expecting to see signs of the War, but the only real signs were the large amount of soldiers everywhere all dressed in khaki. That, and big guns on wheels being hauled along.

I saw a few tanks as well. I'd never seen tanks before. They were huge metal monsters with caterpillar tracks, and big guns poking out. It was said they could crawl over any sort of mud and just keep firing, the shots from the enemy would just bounce off the metal casing.

"Not much sign of any fighting," said Wally, looking disappointed.

"Don't worry, you'll find it soon enough all right," said another soldier who was pushing his way through the crowded train. "And if you don't, it'll find you."

When we reached St Omer we were transferred to buses taking us to a smaller town called Poperinghe.

"How d'you spell that?" Danny asked an older soldier.

"Why d'you want to know how to spell it?" asked the soldier. "This war's about fighting, not about reading."

"I need to know so when I write home to my mum I can tell her where I am," said Danny.

The older soldier laughed out loud.

"What's so funny?" asked Danny, puzzled.

"It's a waste of time putting place names in any letters back home," said the soldier. "They cross 'em out."

"Who do?" asked Alf.

"The army censors," replied the soldier. "It's in case our letters fall into enemy hands. They don't want the Hun knowing where our units are, or what we're doing, do they?"

I was a bit annoyed at the thought of someone else reading my letters home. Letters are supposed to be private. Mind, I could see that what the soldier said made sense.

The village we were headed for, this Poperinghe, was in an area called Passchendaele. It was near a town they said was called Wipers (which I found out later was spelled Ypres and was actually pronounced Eepre).

I kept my eyes on the landscape as our bus rolled along. It was flat country, really flat, made up of green fields with a small wood every now and then. I could see a few houses scattered about here and there in between the fields. It reminded me a bit of the flat part of Cumberland back home, up by the Solway Plain, but even that had more hills than this place.

It was nightfall when we finally got to Poperinghe. There was no time to take a look at the town and get an idea of what it was like: as soon as we got off our bus we were lined up and marched off towards some fields just outside the town where the army had set up camp. Rows and rows of tents stretched for what looked like miles. The Union Jack flew on a flag-pole. In other fields further away I could see other flags flying.

"Australians," nodded Wally, pointing at one of the other flags, which seemed to be stars and a small Union Jack on a blue flag. "I recognize the flag 'cos I've got an uncle who lives out there."

"Maybe he'll be over here with the Australian troops?" suggested Danny.

"Unlikely," said Wally. "He's 70 years old."

We were assigned six men to a tent, and our group snaffled a tent quick so that we could all be together. We'd each grabbed a bunk and were starting to sort our gear out, when a soldier from another unit poked his head into our tent.

"New arrivals?" he asked.

"Aye," said Charlie. "Just got here."

"Well, in a minute the bugle's going to blow for food, so if you want to make sure you get there among the first, take my tip and head over to the mess tent right now."

With that he gave us a wink, then hurried off.

"Food!" sighed Alf. "About time! Come on, lads, let's get over there!"

The six of us hurried towards the mess tent. Signs had been put up pointing out where it was. Also, the smell of food cooking was wafting over the camp, so we just followed our noses.

Until I sat down at a long wooden trestle table with a plate of stew and mashed potato, I hadn't realized how hungry I was. I hadn't sat down to a proper meal since just before getting on the boat at Folkestone. We'd grabbed some food at Boulogne, and then again at St Omer while we were waiting for our bus, but this was our first proper meal since leaving England. I wolfed down my food in a state of excitement. I was in Belgium with my mates, ready to start winning the War!

After mess, it was back to the tent and lights out, and sleep. Not that I could really get to sleep. After the long journey I'd had, all the way from Yorkshire, I thought I'd be worn out and ready to sleep, but my mind was in a whirl. All I could think of was that I was finally here, ready for battle. What would it be like at the Front? What would we be doing as Engineers?

Next morning the six of us loaded up our packs and joined the column of men heading for the Front. Our column was about 100 men strong, and made up of men from different regiments, some going to fighting units in the trenches, others – like us – being sent to support units. The routine, our Sergeant told us, was seven days in the front-line trenches, followed by seven days back at our billets, then seven days in the trenches again, and so on. We were being thrown in at the deep end straight away, off for our first week at the very heart of the battle.

We marched towards the Front along roads made of cobbles. The nearer we got to the Front, the worse the roads became, the cobbles sinking into mud and disappearing beneath the surface, until in the end we were marching as best we could on a potholed muddy track.

We were lucky that our training back home had made us fit, because the weight we had to carry on our backs in our haversacks made the marching even more difficult. As Engineers, we didn't have rifles and ammunition to weigh us down, but in their places we had bigger and heavier picks and shovels, as well as our mess tin and our water bottle. We also had our gas mask, which we'd been told might one day save our lives, so I made sure mine was within easy grabbing distance.

We Engineers were near the back of the column, and I couldn't help a feeling of envy when I looked at the fighting men marching in front of us. That was where I wanted to be. Armed and ready to fight. Not for the first time, I wondered how Rob was doing out here. Had he killed his first Hun yet?

After miles of marching our legs and shoulders ached, but as we neared the Front we could hear the booming sounds of heavy guns in the distance, and even at this range we could feel the ground shuddering beneath our feet from the heavy shells.

"Looks like we've found the War at last," grinned Charlie,

and me and Wally started to chuckle nervously, but we were soon cut short by a yell of, "No talking in the ranks!" from one of the Sergeants just behind us.

We marched on in silence. So this was the Front. I had never seen anything so desolate before. Just a sea of mud as far as the eye could see. Mud and barbed wire, and deep craters. And miles and miles of trenches filled with soldiers. I wondered where our trenches stopped and the German trenches began. Where was the enemy? I felt a knot of excitement in my belly as I craned my head, scanning the horizon for any sign of them.

"Right turn!" came the order from the Sergeant at the front of our column, and we turned off the road and descended into a trench. I'd dug ditches back home but these trenches were deeper than any of them. This one was about 7 feet deep and about 3 feet wide, its stinking clay walls held back by anything that was available: bits of timber, strands of wire, pieces of corrugated iron, sandbags.

Wooden duckboards formed a kind of walkway along the trench, but they were slippery with mud, and in many places they'd broken and sunk under the water. As we made our way along the trench, doing our best to keep our footing, we passed soldiers covered with mud. The holes were filled with freezing cold and stinking water.

"More lambs for the slaughter!" commented one mud-covered soldier as we passed him.

The other soldiers laughed, but their laughter was cut short with a shout from their Sergeant Major, who hollered, "Shut up in the ranks, you lot, or I'll have you all shot for treasonous talk!"

The Royal Engineers were among the first to be dispersed. There were a dozen of us, including Charlie and me, and as we stumbled down the rickety wooden steps into what appeared to be a hole in the ground lit by smoky kerosene lamps, a cheer went up from the grimy soldiers inside the hole.

"Look, lads! Relief is here!" chuckled one.

Charlie looked round at the wet clay walls held up by shafts of timber.

"You'd need to be a rabbit to be able to live here," he said.

"Think yourself lucky we've got somewhere like this," said one of the grimy soldiers. "It's only because we're Engineers. The fighting units don't even have this luxury!"

"Their officers do, Paddy," commented another soldier. "Caves with proper chairs and tables in them. I've seen them."

"Don't mind him, he's just jealous," grinned the soldier called Paddy. "He can't get used to sleeping in muddy water. Anyway, let's get you lot sorted out. Believe me, you're going to be busy!"

Paddy was right. During those first weeks I was busier than I'd ever been in my life.

At the Front there was a complicated system of trenches. Each Infantry trench had two others behind it: a support trench, and then a reserve trench behind that. They were all connected by a communications trench, along which supplies and relief operations were carried out. The telegraph cables were laid along the reserve trench, so the Infantry wouldn't get caught up in them when they went over the top. The whole thing was a bit like a maze, except made out of mud.

Most of our work consisted of repairing lengths of telegraph cables that had been broken during German artillery attacks. The cables were supposed to have been buried at least 6 feet below ground level so they didn't get broken when bombs came down, but the shells the Hun had been using of late were so big they were churning up holes in the mud 10 feet deep. There was only one way to repair a smashed cable when that happened and that was to run new lengths and join them on to the last good bit.

We went out on repair missions and worked in teams of two. My team was Charlie and me. Ginger and Wally were a team, and Danny and Alf were the third. The work was tough. You had to cut through the damaged cable, which was hard because it was covered in steel, lead or brass for added protection, and then make the connections. And all the time you were knee-deep in mud, sometimes waist-deep, and waiting for the Hun to launch another artillery attack, or send over a wave of troops armed with guns with bayonets.

The cables were vital for HQ to keep in contact with the troops at the Front. They'd tried using wireless, but it only really worked between aeroplanes and a ground station. Here in the trenches it was almost impossible. Our side had tried it. There was a thing called the British Field Trench Set, which you were supposed to be able to carry about and pick up and transmit messages. The trouble was it needed at least three men to carry it, and another six to carry the batteries needed to work it.

The Engineers had also recently tried a newer wireless set, the Loop Set. This was a bit more efficient. For one thing its aerial could be attached to a bayonet stuck in the ground, and it didn't need as many men to lug it around. The problem was it only had a range of about 2,000 yards, and lots of the time it just packed up and didn't work. Which meant we Engineers were always busy laying miles and miles of cables to keep communications going.

During my first few days in the trenches I discovered that what Paddy had said about us "living in luxury" in our hole in the ground was right. In our trench a cave had been dug out of the walls to store our equipment and we could use it as a shelter. For the soldiers of the fighting units, only officers had dugouts, ordinary soldiers had to make do with a waterproof sheet for shelter. Some of them had scraped small holes in the walls of the trench themselves, just large enough to fit in one man sitting down, but it didn't give much protection either from the elements or from shrapnel. These were known as "funk holes" and the only advantage they offered was that a soldier had a clay seat to sit on and a bit of muddy cover when waiting for action, rather than squatting in a deep puddle of icy muddy water in the open.

I was told by soldiers who'd been in the trenches for some time that this was a quiet patch. It didn't seem quiet to me. Every time Charlie and me and the other Engineers went out the Germans seemed to be shelling our positions. The first few days I spent most of my time throwing myself into the walls of the trenches, waiting to be hit by a bomb, or by flying shrapnel. Now I knew why soldiers were covered in mud from head to foot.

The first time I heard a high explosive going off it was terrifying. It makes an ear-splitting roar and the world around you shakes violently. Every time I expected the walls of the trench to fall in. Mostly the clay stuck together and held, but sometimes a crack would appear and a thick slice of clay, several feet thick, would topple over and fill in the trench, covering everything beneath it.

Shrapnel was the really terrifying thing. Bits of metal of different sizes, some large, some small, exploding out of a shell and hurtling through the air at incredible speed, slicing through anything in their way.

The mules and horses that hauled the gun carriages and the supply wagons were often caught in the bombing. On my first day I saw two of these poor animals with their legs destroyed by shrapnel, screaming with pain in the mud until they were put out of their misery by a bullet in their head.

On my second day out repairing cables, I saw my first dead man. His head was out of sight, covered in mud. All I could see was the remains of an arm and some ribs, with rotting flesh and bits of uniform sticking to it. Maggots were coming out from the hole in his ribs. I took one look at him and was sick.

"Get it out," said Charlie, patting me on the back as I vomited. "You'll see worse than this before this is over."

The sight of that dead soldier made me think of Rob and Jed and the rest of my old mates from the Lonsdales. I wondered how they were. Had any of them been wounded, or killed? I felt a sinking feeling in my stomach at the thought that, all the time I'd been feeling jealous of Rob because he was with a fighting unit, he might have actually been wounded in the fighting. Or, even worse, been killed. The thought made me shiver.

When we were out working we had to be alert for gas, especially mustard gas. We were told that the Germans also used chlorine and phosgene gas, which got into your lungs and filled them up with water so you drowned. But mustard gas was the worst of all.

Mustard gas didn't have a smell to warn you, it just crept up on you and next thing you knew you were retching and coughing and blinded, your eyes burning. It killed you by filling your lungs and burning you from the inside. The only defence against gas was the respirator, a weird-looking mask that you pulled on over your face. It had big goggles over your eyes and a hose like an elephant's trunk coming down to the canister on your front. But those funny-looking respirators saved many men's lives.

Then there were the rats. I'd seen rats back home in Cumberland, but these trench rats were as big as cats. I was told they fed off the bodies of the men who were left to rot in the muddy waters of the trenches. They had become so used to sharing the trenches with us soldiers that they didn't run away and hide like rats back home, they walked about quite openly. So you had to make sure that your rations were well and truly hidden away inside your mess tin, otherwise you'd find a rat had got in and eaten them.

With all of this, at the end of my first seven days in the trenches, I was more than ready when the order came for us to return to our billets at Poperinghe.

"It's a long walk back!" complained Charlie as we trudged our way along the muddy track.

"True, but at least we'll be in a bed tonight," I said. "And for the next six nights after that."

"Quiet back there!" shouted our Sergeant Major. "No talking in the ranks!"

We shut up and marched. Or, rather, trudged. After

seven days and nights in the trenches we were all weary, battle-shocked and sore. I noticed that the numbers of the men coming back from the fighting units were fewer than had come out, and for the first time it struck me that I might be lucky that I was with the Engineers rather than the Infantry.

When we arrived back at our billets and were given the order to "Dismiss!", Charlie took the opportunity to head for the latrines before they got too full. I headed straight for the bathhouse, aiming to get some of the muck off, and get rid of the lice.

Charlie and I realized we'd caught lice after we'd been in the trenches for just two days. That first night I realized I'd got them I'd stripped off all my clothes as soon as I got back to our dugout and started searching for them by the light of a kerosene lamp and began picking them off my skin. It was a waste of time. What I didn't know was that lice laid their eggs in the seams of your clothes, so you could pick off as many as you liked, but more would come as soon as you put your clothes back on. You just had to get used to the fact that lice lived off you, eating at your skin under your clothes, and all you could do was try not to scratch or you'd just make the sores on your skin worse.

Because the problems of lice were so bad, a Delousing Station had been set up for the troops at Poperinghe. It was an old converted brewery.

The Delousing Station was full of men like me who'd just come back from their week in the trenches, all covered with mud. I followed their example. I stripped off and tied my uniform and my underwear into a bundle, and then tied my hat and boots to it.

My clothes were put into a fumigator along with everyone else's. Then I followed the others, all naked and with their skin covered in blotches and bites from the lice, into the delousing area.

The three large vats that they once used to brew beer in were full of water. The water in the first one was hot and soapy, but very, very dirty. It looked more like soup. Along with a bunch of other men I stepped in and jumped up and down a bit, letting the hot water get into my skin.

"Come on, no hanging about," complained a voice behind me. "There's others waiting."

I took the hint. I grabbed hold of the rope that was hung across the vats and pulled myself along to the other side. Then I climbed out and got into the next vat. The water was hot and not quite so dirty. After that it was into the third vat – and the shock of freezing cold water.

I got out quickly and towelled myself as dry as I could, and collected my clothes, which now stank of smoke and disinfectant.

Once I was cleaned up, I went off to our billet and collected Charlie and the others, and we set off for

Poperinghe, and the place where I'd been told all the soldiers went for relaxation, Marguerite's café.

The place looked tiny from the outside, but inside it seemed to go on for ever. And it was packed with blokes in khaki. The air was thick with smoke from cigarettes. And the noise! Soldiers singing and laughing. Looking at this lot it was hard to think there was a war on. It was very different to the pubs back home in Carlisle. They were places for serious drinking of beer. This place was more like a cafeteria or a club.

Ginger, Wally, Danny and Alf hurried straight in, heading for the bar, while Charlie and I stood just inside the entrance looking for a table, when I heard a familiar voice call out, "Billy! Over here!" I turned, and there was Rob! He was sitting at a table in one corner of the café where Jed Lowe and a couple of other blokes from the Lonsdales were sitting.

I waved at him, and Charlie and me began to battle our way through the crowd to the table. Rob had managed to grab a couple of empty chairs.

I made the introductions, and Charlie and Rob and the others shook hands.

"This is amazing, Rob!" I said. "I was thinking about you, wondering how you were!"

"As you can see, still alive," grinned Rob.

"How long have you been out here?" I asked.

"About four weeks," replied Rob. "We're going back to

the Front tomorrow." He looked around at the smoky, noisy café and said, "You'll like this place, Billy. They do really great chips. Not as good as back home in Carlisle, but still very good. That is, if you can catch the waiter's eye."

He poured Charlie and me a glass of white wine.

"Here you are, try some of this," said Rob.

"No beer?" asked Charlie.

"Yeah, but this stuff's cheaper," said Rob. "*Vin rouge* or *vin blanc*. Red or white. Take your choice." He grinned. "Listen to me. Only been here four weeks and I'm talking French like a native."

For the rest of the evening, against the noise of soldiers at other tables around us playing cards, or dominoes, and a local man playing popular songs on his old accordion, Rob and I caught up.

I wanted to know what it was like in the Infantry, but Rob said he'd prefer to leave the trenches back at the Front where they belonged and concentrate on what I'd been up to.

Of course, my experiences had been much the same as his, but without a rifle and going into attack. We'd both spent most of the time up to our knees in muddy water.

I did learn that there didn't seem to be much of an advance going on, either by our side or by the Germans.

"A stalemate, that's what it is," said Rob, sipping at his wine. "Our lot lob bombs at them. Their lot lob bombs at us. Then sometimes we go over the top and charge at them, and then we come back again. And sometimes they charge at us, and then they go back again. Or, at least, the lucky ones do." And his face darkened as the memories of the battlefield came back to him. "Lots never make it back. Their bodies just lie there, in the middle of No Man's Land. Too many of them to go out and bring back. And if you tried you'd only end up there yourself." Then he smiled again and the shadow on his brow vanished. "Still, forget that. Let's get back to you. What's it like being in the Royal Engineers?"

And so I told him of my training, and the classes I'd had to go to back in England. Yet here I was, still digging trenches.

"Think yourself lucky you are," grinned Rob. "You wouldn't like it in the Infantry. Apart from the fact the Hun keep shooting at us every time we pop our heads over the top of the trench, our Sergeant Major is worse than old Mr Dickens back at school. Shouts and hollers like he's angrier with us than he is with the Germans!"

And so the night went on, until finally the man playing the accordion stopped and a woman shouted out, "*Allez! Allez!*", which I was told meant "Time to go home".

And so we went back to barracks. "I'll see you, old pal," said Rob when we got back to camp, and Charlie and I were heading off for our billets.

I shook his hand. "Take care of yourself, Rob," I said. "And we'll keep in touch whenever we can."

"With lots more nights like tonight at Marguerite's," grinned Rob.

All too soon our leave was over, and we were back in the trenches. Just after midnight on 6 June we were all summoned to assemble for a briefing.

"A briefing at midnight!" snorted Charlie. "Why couldn't they tell us what they've got to tell us at a reasonable hour, instead of us having to scramble about in the mud in the dark?"

"Got to be some sort of top secret," suggested Wally. "They don't want the Germans to see us all standing in line in the trenches and giving the game away that something's up."

We filed out of our cave and lined up with the rest of the men in our reserve trench, where our Commanding Officer, Lieutenant Jackson, addressed us. I felt we were lucky because Lieutenant Jackson was all right. He wasn't friendly with us and he kept his distance, which suited us fine, but he wasn't like some of the officers I'd seen. They treated the soldiers under them like they were schoolkids, or like they were prisoners who were under constant punishment.

"Men," he said, "a major offensive is about to be launched on the Messines Ridge at just after 0300 hours. Although the ridge is some distance away from us, we will all be affected, because just before the offensive a series of explosions will be set off beneath the German lines. You will all feel the shock waves and they will be larger than you are used to. They will be nothing to worry about. However, we have been instructed that it will be considered safest if, when the explosives are detonated, all men are in full view in the trench and not in a dugout. Dismissed, and carry on about your duties."

Me, Charlie, Wally, Danny, Ginger and Alf scrambled back inside our cave where we were fixing cable lengths together.

"The Messines Ridge is miles away to the south," commented Danny. "I can't see why we have to stand out in the trench just because they're letting off a few explosions. It won't affect us."

As most of the others nodded, I noticed that Alf was looking thoughtful.

"What's the matter, Alf?" I asked. "You look worried."

"No, I was just thinking," said Alf. "I don't think this is going to be just any old explosion. It's going to be a big one."

The tone of his voice made us all look at him, surprised. Alf wasn't one for making up stories. As a rule he didn't say a lot.

"What makes you say that?" asked Danny.

Alf hesitated, and I threw in, "Come on, Alf, you've said

enough to whet our appetites. We're your mates. If something big's going to be happening in less than three hours and it affects us, and you know about it, you ought to tell us."

Ginger, Wally, Charlie and Danny all nodded in agreement.

"OK," said Alf. "But first, go out and check that there's no one outside listening. I don't want to get arrested for betraying official secrets."

"It's not an official secret any more," I pointed out. "Lieutenant Jackson's just told us all it's all going to happen at 0300 hours. So what's the secrecy for?"

Alf wasn't convinced. He had to go to the entrance of our cave and look up and down the trench to make sure there was no one outside listening, before he came back and started to tell us what he knew.

"Just before I left home to go training I met up with my Uncle Harry. He was a coalminer back home and one night he was telling us about a job he and loads of his miner mates had been sent on, but because it was all Top Secret he wasn't supposed to tell anyone."

"So why did he tell you?" I asked, puzzled.

Alf gave a rueful sigh. "Because Uncle Harry can't keep a secret," he said. "He talks all the time. Drives my Aunt Ethel mad."

"Forget about your Aunt Ethel, get back to what he told you," said Charlie impatiently.

"Right," said Alf. "Well, according to Uncle Harry the army were digging tunnels under this place in Belgium called Messines Ridge. They needed coalminers instead of just ordinary soldiers. From Wales, Yorkshire, Nottinghamshire. And not just coalminers. They also brought over all these cockneys from London, the ones who'd built the London underground, because they were also used to digging tunnels in clay."

I looked around at the dripping wet walls of our cave and shivered at the thought of digging deep underground in this muck.

"I wouldn't fancy doing that job," I said.

"You might when you hear what Uncle Harry told us they were being paid. Six shillings a day."

"Six shillings!" said Charlie, outraged, so loudly that we had to tell him to shut up. I must admit I felt a bit annoyed when I heard that as well. After all, we were only paid one shilling a day.

"And how many of these tunnels are there?" I asked.

"Twenty, so Uncle Harry said. And each one packed with high explosives."

"That's a lot of explosives," I commented.

"A million tons, Uncle Harry reckoned."

We exchanged horrified looks. One million tons of explosives packed into twenty tunnels under the German lines.

"No," said Charlie, shaking his head. "I don't believe it. They couldn't do that much tunnelling without the Germans finding out. They'd hear the work going on. The drilling machines, for one thing."

"No," Alf shook his head. "Uncle Harry said they couldn't use drilling machines in case the Germans heard the sound of the machinery, so they tunnelled using just picks and shovels. The only machines they had were pumps to pump the water out, otherwise they would have drowned."

"If what your Uncle Harry says is true, I'm not sure I want to be in a trench when it all goes up," said Danny. "I think I'd rather be on the top. At least the walls won't be able to fall in on me."

At 0300 hours me, Charlie, Ginger, Wally, Danny and Alf lined up in the trench with the rest of our unit and waited, all looking south towards Messines Ridge. Not that we could see anything because the top of the trench was another foot above our heads, and none of us fancied poking our heads over the top to see what was happening. Knowing what I knew made me feel a knot tighten in my stomach.

The minutes ticked by. 0301. 0302. 0303. And nothing happened. 0304. 0305. Still nothing.

"I bet they've forgotten to connect the detonators," muttered Charlie, and we all laughed.

0309, and still nothing.

And then, at exactly 0310, the whole world heaved upwards, lifting us with it. In a split second it settled down again, but continued to shake. I felt as if I was on a boat that had just hit a big wave. Danny had actually fallen over from the shock of the blast and was picking himself up out of the mud. The shock was so huge I bet they even felt it as far away as London.

Even though it was the middle of the night we could see as clearly as if it was broad daylight. The whole sky just lit up, a huge mass of flames reaching upwards. For a minute we all just stood there, looking at one another. My body was still shaking.

"Good old Uncle Harry," muttered Charlie.

And then, seconds later, our big guns opened up. The barrage was deafening even from this many miles away. About five minutes after the big guns had stopped, there came the sounds of distant whistles. In the trenches at the Front, our Infantry were going over the top.

The attack that followed carried on for three days, driving for about a mile through the lines of shattered Germans, until our boys came up against stronger Hun defences, which stopped them, making them dig in.

We found out afterwards that in the attack over 5,000 Germans were taken prisoner. Most of them had been so stunned by the explosion they didn't know what day it was, or where they were. It was like killing fish by dropping dynamite into a pool.

But the Huns started to fight back. Bombardment after bombardment came over at us from the German lines. Shells rained down on our trenches. Our workload increased as they scored hits on our communication cables.

After one raid, Charlie and I were sent out to repair yet another broken telegraph cable in yet another water-filled trench, this one even closer to the German lines. One look at the cable told us it was smashed beyond repair. It would have to be replaced.

We rolled the huge reel of replacement cable along the trench as best we could in the mud, then we set about hauling out a length. The only way to stop it from sinking in the mud and disappearing before we'd made the connections was to push the blades of our spades into the clay walls of the trench sides, and then drape the cable over them.

I was pulling at the cable when, suddenly, out of nowhere, something hit the wall of the trench just above us, landing with a sort of plop.

There was another plop, and this time I saw something falling into the mud just near us. For a second I thought it was a grenade and I threw myself backwards, expecting it to go off. Then Charlie started coughing and retching, and I saw him scramble to pull his respirator over his face. In that second I realized what it was and I felt sick to my stomach.

Mustard gas!

A feeling of panic hit me and I scrambled to get my respirator over my face before the killer gas got into my mouth and nose and burnt my lungs. It burned everything it touched. Eyes. Skin. And it always found a way in. Like now, I could feel where it had crept up inside the sleeves of my uniform and the skin on my arms felt like it was on fire. I threw myself into a muddy hole, pushing my arms under water, but I knew it was already too late.

My neck was burning too. My collar must have come undone while I was hauling the cables. It only needed one little opening for the gas to get in, and now I could feel it spreading down the skin on to my chest. Frantically, I pushed myself right up to my goggles in the muddy water, anything to stop the burning, but the water blocked the ventilator outlet for my respirator. My goggles started to mist up and I could feel myself choking.

I stumbled to my feet, saturated, with the weight of wet mud clinging to me. I couldn't move. I couldn't see. I couldn't feel anything except my skin burning. I screamed for help but was stunned by a searing pain in my head. It was as if someone had taken an axe to it and cut it in two.

I woke up to the sound of screaming. There was a smell of blood and rotting flesh mixed with the strong smell of disinfectant.

As the screaming died down I became aware of the

sounds of tin plates being clattered together, and the whispering of voices.

I struggled to open my eyes. My eyelids felt heavy. At first everything looked a bit hazy, but after I blinked a few times my vision started to clear.

I was in a Casualty Station. All around me were men laid out on beds.

I tried to sit up, but the pain in my head made me lay down again. I let out a groan as I fell back on my pillow, which brought a medical orderly over to the side of my bed.

"Awake, are you?" he said cheerfully. "You were lucky."

"What happened?" I asked. My voice felt hoarse, my throat dry.

"A piece of shrapnel caught you," said the orderly. "If you hadn't had your helmet on it might've taken the top of your head clean off. I've seen it happen. Sliced open like a melon."

I looked down at my body and was surprised to see that both my arms were bandaged from fingertip to just above the elbow.

"My arms?" I asked, my voice still a rasp.

"Hang on, I'll give you some water," said the orderly.

He helped me to sit up in the bed and put a tin mug to my lips.

"Here you are," he said. "Get a sip of this."

I sipped at the water. It felt strange. My tongue and lips

and the inside of my mouth seemed to have swollen to twice their normal size.

"There," he said, taking the mug away.

"My arms," I said again. "What happened to my arms?"

"Burns from the mustard gas," replied the orderly. "Like I say, you were very lucky on so many counts. Lucky you were wearing your helmet. Lucky you were wearing your respirator. Lucky you didn't go right under in the mud. Lucky the stretcher party found you. All in all, you are a very lucky young man."

I looked around the Casualty Station at the patients in the beds near me. Many of the men were heavily wrapped up like Egyptian mummies, their bandages soaked in blood.

"Johnson!" barked a man standing by one of the other beds, bandaging a soldier. "I need you here!"

"Coming, sir!" said the orderly, and he trotted off.

It was in my third day in bed in the Casualty Station when a familiar figure walked in, a smile on his face.

"Hello, Billy! Having a nice rest?" It was Charlie.

"Thank heavens you're OK," I said. "I asked the orderly what had happened to you, but no one seemed to know."

"I fell in a hole," said Charlie. "Lucky for me it seemed to keep most of the gas off me. Looks like you caught most of it. And the shrapnel. How's the head?"

"Hurts now and then," I said. "But lucky for me I've

still got a head. Where have you been? Another Casualty Station?"

"No. Still in the trenches at the Front," said Charlie. "I thought, after you copped it, they might let me take a bit of time off, but no. 'The cables won't lay themselves,' they told me. That's why I haven't been able to get in to see you before."

Charlie settled himself down on the rickety chair beside my bed and proceeded to fill me in on what had happened to our unit during the German attack. Apparently I'd come off the worst. Of the other blokes from our unit who'd been working near us, Ginger had been half-drowned in a mud-slide, but nothing too bad. Wally and Danny had got away with just a few scratches and burns from hot shrapnel. They'd all managed to escape from serious gassing.

"Though the Infantry further along the trench weren't so lucky," said Charlie. "That's where most of the gas bombs fell and a lot of them hadn't got their gas mask packed so they could get at it easily. Seems they preferred to keep their rifles and grenades nearer to hand. Some of them got tangled up in all the stuff they were carrying as the gas came down and they couldn't see to find their gas masks. Hundreds of them got caught in it."

"Many dead?" I asked.

Charlie nodded. "Most of 'em. Those that aren't are blind. We were lucky."

"Any news of my mate Rob?" I asked.

Charlie shook his head. "No," he said. "Just that he wasn't one of the casualties. I checked the list they posted just before I came to see you. I thought you'd be worried about him."

"Thanks," I said.

Charlie stayed a bit longer, chatting and telling stories about the other men in our unit, until an orderly came over and told him it was time to go.

"Your talking is disturbing the other patients," the orderly snapped. "This is a Casualty Station, not a café."

Charlie shrugged, gave me a wink, and said: "OK, Billy, looks like I've got my marching orders. I'll see you in a couple of days back in the mud, when they kick you out of here."

I gave him a smile, and after he'd gone I thought about what Charlie had said. A couple more days here in the hospital and I'd be going back to the Front. Back to the mud and the bullets and the barbed wire and the gas, and I knew I didn't want to go back. I wanted to be back at home, back in Carlisle. Back to safety and my job at the railway station and my mum's cooking. But I knew I couldn't. None of us could. We were going to be here until this war was over. Or until we were killed.

As it turned out, Charlie was wrong about me going straight back to the Front. The doctor who examined me the next day told me: "Right, Stevens, we're discharging you. We need your bed. There are injured men waiting to be treated."

"Right, sir," I said.

I indicated the bandages that covered my arms. "Can I have your permission to get something from the stores that will keep these bandages covered in the trenches, though, sir? Otherwise they'll just fall off on the first day, with all the wet and the mud and everything."

"You're not going straight back to the trenches, not with those burns," said the doctor.

I looked at him, puzzled. If I wasn't being sent back to the trenches, then where was I going? Not back home, surely? Men with worse injuries than mine were still fighting out here.

The doctor saw the look on my face, so he explained: "I've arranged for you to go to Base HQ. You can carry on your work as a telegraph operator there. You'll be out of the mud for a while, at least until your skin heals. But don't worry. A week or two and you'll be all right to go back and join your pals."

## JULY 1917

Base HQ was in an old town hall in St Omer. It reminded me of some of the town halls back in England, or the big old libraries. It was an enormous building, made of blocks of stone, and inside it was absolutely spick-and-span clean. You could have eaten your dinner off the floor of the entrance lobby. It was such an amazing contrast after the dirt and mess of life in the trenches, or even back at camp in Poperinghe.

The big entrance lobby had a marble floor that made an echoing sound when I walked in and the soles of my boots hit the marble. It made me feel like I ought to tiptoe and whisper, just like I used to when I was in the Town Hall back home in Carlisle.

I went to the desk and gave my name and the piece of paper they'd given me at the Casualty Station, and was sent immediately to see the man who'd be my officer while I was here, Sergeant MacWilliams. The Sergeant told me that I was to replace the regular telegraph operator who had been sent back home on leave. Then he told me how I was to act while I was here.

"Here, Stevens, you are like the three wise monkeys.

You see nothing, you hear nothing, and you say nothing. Is that clear?"

"Yes, Sarge," I said.

"Good. Because if word gets back to me – and it will, believe me – that you've said one word of what goes on in this place, or repeated what's been said to anybody, I'll make sure you're shot for treason. Is that clear?"

He then called for another private to show me where I would be based.

I couldn't believe the luxury of it! All right, it was in a wooden hut that had been set up in the grounds at the back of the building, but I had a real bunk, with real sheets and pillows.

After weeks of sleeping on a rickety cot, or trying to sleep in a mud-hole in the trenches, this was like being in heaven. That night I had the best night's sleep I'd had in ages.

And then there was the food at Base HQ. Hot dinners. Real meat and potatoes with gravy. Back at the Front we never saw a hot meal from one day till the next, not unless we could cook it ourselves over the flame of a kerosene lamp. And finding something edible to cook in the trenches was hard. Because of the rats everything had to be kept in tins. So we had tins of meat, usually bully beef, which was just stewed beef pressed into tins. Then there were tins of vegetable stew that tasted like nothing I'd ever had at home. And hard biscuits that were more like dog biscuits.

So I was shocked when I heard some of the officers at Base HQ complaining because they couldn't get the food they liked. "No grouse. No venison," complained one. "How can a man live?"

I just kept my head down and my mouth shut and wondered what they'd say if they had to live on bully beef and dog biscuits like most of us in the trenches.

Next day I started work, operating the telegraph keys, receiving and transmitting messages using Morse code. My key for sending messages was like a small metal knob balanced on a spring on a piece of flat board. This was connected to an electric cable. When I pressed this key down, it completed the electric circuit. I could send messages to another telegraph operator by tapping this key, quickly for a "dot", a bit longer for a "dash". Different combinations of dots and dashes represented different words.

I received messages using a sounder key, which was a small brass arm on a pivot. When it was pressed down, it also completed an electric circuit, and I could receive messages, printed out on long strips of paper.

Because it took so long for a message to come through this way, they tended to be short, using as few words as possible. It also took a good memory to know what each of the symbols stood for, without having to keep looking them up. Being the one who could translate the coded messages meant that I saw all the information that came in and went out, and I quickly realized what the Sergeant had meant about seeing nothing and hearing nothing, and keeping my mouth shut.

And it wasn't just the messages. All the Top Brass came through this building, and once they were inside the building they all talked about the War and how it was going, and what the plans were. It was as if we lower ranks were deaf and couldn't hear them, or couldn't understand what they were talking about. Or maybe they just didn't notice us. I'd noticed that about some rich people, they talk about all sorts of private things when the servants are around, things they'd never talk about in front of other people of their same class. I suppose servants are sort of invisible to them; they're people who don't count so they don't notice them.

With all these field marshals and brigadiers and generals around, and messages going backwards and forwards on the telegraph, I learnt more about the War than I'd have ever found out if I'd asked one of the officers from my own unit. I expect that if I had asked questions about what the plans were, and how the War was really going, I'd have been court-martialled as a spy. But officers talked about these things in the same room as me, or gave me messages to send, or receive, with all this important information.

One thing that really seemed to have the Top Brass worried was what was happening in Russia. Earlier in the year there'd been a revolution there and a new People's Government had taken over the country. The ordinary people of Russia were fed up with the way they were treated by the rich people.

The Top Brass were worried that Russia might pull out of the War. If this happened, the Germans would be able to release their troops from the Russian Front and send them to back up their troops here in Flanders.

But they were more worried that the ordinary people in Britain, especially us troops, might hear about the revolution and decide to start one of our own. In our trenches and at camp we'd heard rumours that there had already been mutinies among the French soldiers over bad food, terrible living conditions and no leave. I reckoned that the Top Brass were right to be worried.

I thought about what life was like for me and Charlie and the others in the trenches. And about Rob and Jed Lowe and all the other fighting units going over the top and being cut down, and I couldn't help but feel that Base HQ and the way the generals lived was a long way from what the War was really like. The dirt and the bullets and the blood and the mud. But I didn't say it out loud.

I also found out that not all the Top Brass agreed with the way the War was being fought. A lot of the generals wanted a quick end to the War and I heard one say to another that the Commander-in-chief ought to go for one all-out attack and finish the Germans off and get it over and done with. Messages came through from London, from the Secretary to the Prime Minister, saying much the same thing. But then I overheard General Plumer, who was the Commander's right-hand man, say to one of his major generals that the Commander's view was "to wear down the Hun bit by bit, like a dripping tap". He added: "It's not worth throwing our weight against the Hun while he's still strong. We've got to weaken him first before we strike with everything we've got."

When I heard this I thought, "That's all very well, but back in the trenches we're throwing everything we've got at the Germans already and they seem to be as strong as ever." But I didn't say it out loud, I kept my mouth shut.

I'd been at Base HQ for about four days when the Commander-in-chief himself, Field Marshal Sir Douglas Haig, arrived. He'd been on a tour of his commanders at their different positions at the Front to see how the War was going. He came into the Communications Room with General Plumer and immediately Sergeant MacWilliams leapt out of his chair and snapped stiffly to attention, banging the heels of his boots smartly together, saluting as he did so. I followed his lead and leapt to my feet, snatching off my earphones.

I was amazed to find that Haig was much smaller than I'd thought he'd be. I don't know why I expected him to be tall, but I did. His hair was white, and he had a big moustache. He carried himself absolutely stiff and straight.

"Stand easy, Sergeant," said Plumer.

Sergeant MacWilliams and I stood easy, and the Sergeant

gave me a hard look which meant "Get back to work", so I sat down, put my earphones back on and turned back to my telegraph key.

"Any messages, Sergeant?" asked Plumer.

"All today's messages have gone to Brigadier General Davidson, sir!" bellowed the Sergeant.

That was one of the odd things about sergeants, they seemed to shout all the time, even when they were talking to someone just a few feet away.

Haig and Plumer nodded, then turned and walked out of the room. In the whole time Haig hadn't said one word.

Sergeant MacWilliams turned to me and said: "You are a very privileged man, Stevens. You have just seen one of the greatest men in the world. If we had more men like Field Marshal Haig this war would be over by Christmas."

The day after Field Marshal Haig arrived a new phrase started to crop up in messages that I sent and received. "Big Push". At first I hadn't got the faintest idea what this meant, and I'd learnt that it didn't do to ask questions. Over the next couple of days, though, I kept my eyes and ears open trying to find out more about it. I soon learnt from the mutterings that went on between generals and brigadiers and other officers, that this Big Push was going to be a major offensive. No one said when it was going to be, or where it was going to be, but a decision had definitely been taken to launch a massive all-out assault.

I was surprised, especially after what I'd heard General Plumer say about "the dripping tap" and that Haig didn't believe in launching a major offensive until the Germans were already weakened. From the telegraph messages that I was taking the Germans seemed as strong as ever. It occurred to me that maybe the Commander wasn't the one taking the big decisions. But then, if Field Marshal Haig wasn't, who *was* taking the decisions? Was it the politicians back in London? I'd heard rumours that there had been a lot of arguments between Haig and the Prime Minister, David Lloyd George, about how this war was being run. A couple of days later I heard solid proof.

I was in the Communications Room, taking down messages that were coming in from stations at the Front, when I heard Field Marshal Haig and General Plumer talking together in the corridor just outside my door. They were talking about the Americans coming into the War. So far, although the Canadians and the New Zealanders and the Australians had come into the War on our side, the Americans had kept out of it and stayed neutral. Charlie and some of the others said this was because there were so many Germans living in America that the Yanks wouldn't know which side to fight on if they came in.

"The first contingent of Americans have arrived in France," I heard Plumer's voice say.

"How many?" came Haig's question.

"Just a few hundred," said Plumer.

"A few hundred!" exploded Haig. "What does President Wilson think this is? A tea party that's got out of control?"

"The Americans say it's just a token force," said Plumer. "They say most of their men are in training and they'll be over here by Christmas."

"Before Christmas!" snapped Haig. "We need them now, not by Christmas! It's bad enough that Lloyd George has taken our planes just to make sure he gets votes! Now he won't ask Wilson to bring his men in earlier! Sometimes I don't think that fool Lloyd George wants us to win this war!"

Then I heard the heels of their boots ringing as they both marched off along the corridor.

The business of the planes I'd only found out about since I'd been at Base HQ. It seems that the Germans had sent over planes and carried out air raids on Britain. The month before, in June, a bomber had scored a direct hit on an infants' school and killed all the little kids. The public back home had been up in arms, demanding to know what the Government was doing to protect it from more German air raids. As a result, the War Cabinet had ordered two squadrons of the Royal Flying Corps to be sent back to England to defend it against German bombers. This meant that the numbers of British planes here in Flanders had been cut and all the generals had been livid.

"We're losing thousands of men a day over here!" I'd heard

one general rage to another. "They lose a few kids and we have to send our flying boys back to protect them. Next thing they'll demand our army goes back to protect them as well!"

Personally, I was glad I was just an ordinary soldier and didn't have to make decisions about where to send the planes or the troops. It seemed to me that whatever the Top Brass did was wrong. If they refused to send planes back to defend England and bombing raids killed more kids, then they'd be in the wrong. But if they sent the planes back to England and our troops were killed because they didn't have protection, they'd be wrong again.

## August 1917

At the end of three weeks, the bloke I had been filling in for at Base HQ returned from leave. By this time, by keeping my skin dry, my burns had healed enough for me to be classed as fit to return to active service. I still had scars on my arms where the skin had been burnt, but many men had worse souvenirs of this war.

I had mixed feelings about going back to the Front. On the down side, after the safety and luxury of life at Base HQ, including a real bed and proper hot food, I was going back to an uncomfortable cot in a tent on a muddy field. Then back into the real mud of the trenches. But I was really looking forward to getting back together with Charlie and the others. Always having to be on my guard about what I might say while I was at HQ, which mainly meant saying nothing at all, had been wearing me down. I never felt relaxed the whole time I was there. It sounds ridiculous that I could feel more relaxed back at the Front, with bombs falling and the Hun firing at us, and the mud and the mess, but I did. And that was because I didn't feel relaxed surrounded by generals and brigadiers, but I did when I was with my own mates.

I managed to squeeze on to one of the transit buses taking the new influx of troops to Poperinghe, and got back to camp by late afternoon.

Charlie was in our tent playing cards with Ginger and Wally as I came in. They all let out a cheer as I walked in.

"Here comes the General!" chuckled Charlie. "Fresh from HQ. Give us a word, General. What are your orders for us ordinary soldiers!"

"You can poke your head in a mud-hole!" I responded with a grin.

The others laughed, and then all started asking questions at once, eager to find out what life was like at Base HQ. Did the generals really eat their food off silver plates? Did they have servants? Was it true they could actually telephone their families back home whenever they wanted? And could they go off on leave every few weeks?

"Later, later!" I protested. "Don't forget, I'm a man who's suffered. I've been forced to eat hot food and lay in a bed with a comfortable pillow and clean cotton sheets. And I've had to have hot baths and wear clean clothes."

Ginger laughed and picked up his pillow, a wet mass of straw, and threw it at me.

I looked round the tent. "Where are Danny and Alf?" I asked. "On leave?"

A silence fell, and then Ginger said awkwardly, "They were both killed."

"How?" I asked weakly.

"Blown to smithereens," said Ginger soberly. "Shrapnel killed Alf. No one knew where Danny was at first, there was so little left of him. He must've taken the whole force of the blast. The people who were first on the scene thought he might have been buried under the mud. Then they found bits all over the place. One of them was Danny's hand. They only knew it was his because of his ring."

I sat there stunned. Alf and Danny killed. One minute alive, the next second … dead.

We'd all seen men killed and all felt bad for them, but when it happened to someone I'd spent time with, worked with, had fun with, it hit me hard.

As well as Danny and Alf, I discovered that another six of the original dozen Engineers had been killed in the last few weeks. Me, Charlie, Ginger and Wally were the only ones left.

"They're bringing out new boys to replace them," said Wally. "They should be here the day after tomorrow. Till then, it's up to us to keep the communications of this war up and running."

I'd been so looking forward to getting back together with my old mates, and now I found two of my closest pals had been killed. I couldn't help but think about Rob. Was he still alive?

The next day me, Charlie, Wally and Ginger returned to the trenches. Because our battalion had been so reduced in numbers we were attached to another unit of Royal Engineers. Two new lads were put with us to make up our unit of six: Terry Crow and Peter Parks. They were both from London, both in their early twenties, fresh out from training. Like all of us, they were trained-up telegraph operators.

In the trenches there was definitely a feeling that something big was about to happen. We could all tell that something was up. For one thing, there seemed to be more soldiers than before. Also, more trenches seemed to have sprung up in the time I'd been away, and they had been dug much nearer to the German lines. All those messages I'd taken and sent while I was at Base HQ, and all those conversations I'd overhead about the "Big Push", started to fall into place. Our Top Brass needed to get on and do something big to win this war, and soon.

Each time Charlie and I went out to repair cables or lay new ones, we were being sent further and further into No Man's Land, the patch of open ground between our front line and the German front line. We were putting more and more cables and telegraph points in the forward trenches, and more and more troops were being moved into them. Seven days passed, then two weeks, and we were still in the trenches, still working.

Then it started to rain. We'd been living with a steady drizzle for some time now, but this was different. This was heavy rain which made the mud we were in even more of a quagmire. Walking through it was like trying to walk through thick glue.

All the time the Germans were pounding at our trenches with their heavy artillery, as if they also knew that something big was about to take place and were doing their best to stop it happening.

At night the Germans sent up flares to light up No Man's Land so they could show up any surprise attack that might be launched. Charlie and I and the other Engineers sat in our dugout in the reserve trench and watched the night sky light up as each new flare went up from the German lines.

And all the time it kept on raining.

One afternoon, just after the middle of September, even more troops filed along the reserve trench, heading for the Front. Charlie and I were in the trench at the time, trying to dig a reel of cable out of a shell-hole. As they passed I recognized one of them. It was my old friend, Jed Lowe from the Lonsdales.

I hailed him, and then looked further along the line of men, and sure enough I picked out the figure of Rob.

"Rob!" I called. He saw me, and stopped and shook my hand.

"Billy," he said. But this time I noticed there was no twinkle in his eyes, no smile on his face. His eyes looked deeper set in his face. He looked so much older than when I had last seen him, even though it had only been two months before.

I jerked my head towards the German lines.

"Looks like this could be it, at last," I said. "The final push."

"I hope so," he said. "Unless the rain stops it."

"Rain stops play," I said, and he almost smiled.

I looked along the line at the soldiers with Rob, and

noticed that on many of them their badges and flashes were all different.

"The Lonsdales changed their badges?" I asked, trying to keep the conversation positive.

Rob grinned wryly. "Not many of us Lonsdales left now, Billy," he said. "I reckon just me and Jed Lowe and half a dozen others are all that's left. We're a combined battalion now. A mixture of us, added with some of the survivors from the Sussex, Middlesex and Hereford Regiments. We call ourselves the Allsorts."

"And how are things in the new unit?" I asked.

Rob shot a quick glance ahead, and then said quietly but angrily: "The men are great, but the new officers who've been sent out are awful. We're told what to do by idiots who don't know the first thing about it. They come out here as officers just because their dad owns a factory or something, and they haven't got a clue about how to mount an attack. We've lost more men because of the stupidity of some of our junior officers than because of German bullets."

"No talking along there!" barked a voice from ahead.

I looked towards the voice and saw a young man who could only have been about twenty himself with a small moustache doing its best to sprout from under his nose.

"Come on, men!" he snapped.

Rob rolled his eyes to show what he thought of his new officer. Then he and the bedraggled troops, with what few remained of the Lonsdale Battalion, trudged forward splish-splashing through the mud. As I watched him go my heart felt heavy. The Rob Matthews who was walking away from me wasn't the Rob I'd known all my life, a happy, positive, optimistic boy. Instead he was an angry and disillusioned young man.

That night, me, Charlie, Wally, Ginger, Terry and Peter tried to get some shut-eye in our dugout cave in our reserve trench. As always, we took turns to keep watch, just in case something happened that meant we had to swing into action. Usually we drew straws to see who took first watch, the one who drew the shortest straw taking it, but this time I volunteered. I didn't think I'd be able to sleep, anyway, my mind was full of what was about to happen. The Big Push that was coming. I thought of Rob and Jed and the remaining Lonsdales, waiting in the front-line trenches for the order to go over the top. They'd be getting their rum ration about now. The men in the front lines, the fighting units, were given a tot of rum each to "warm them up" just before the whistles went and they scaled the ladders and then ran forward to attack the enemy.

At 0200 I woke Wally and he took over on watch, and I crawled on to my bed and tried to get some sleep. I really didn't think I'd be able to sleep with all the thoughts that were in my head, but I suppose the tiredness got to me, because the next thing I remember was Charlie shaking me. It was 0430 hours.

"Time to get up," he said. "They're getting ready."

I scrambled out of our dugout and into the reserve trench. In the darkness I could hear the sounds of activity from the forward trenches: scaling ladders being put into place against the walls; the clicking of rifles being made ready.

"Not long now," said Ginger.

At 0540 our big guns opened up. The ground around us shook and I thought the trench might come down on top of us, despite all the timber holding it up. Even from our trench we saw that over the German lines the sky seemed to be on fire as shell after shell landed on the German positions and blew up.

As well as the heavy guns lobbing shells at the German lines, there was the chatter chatter chatter of our machine-guns opening up, pouring a stream of deadly lead towards the German Front. Then suddenly the machine-guns went quiet and there were the sounds of whistles from ahead of us, and the roar of men's voices as the Infantry went over the top of the trenches and hurled themselves at the German lines. As I huddled in the dugout I thought of Rob and Jed and the rest of the remaining Lonsdales out there in the mud and the infernal noise of No Man's Land, with the Germans firing at them.

The sounds of battle went on for what seemed like hours. Only at daybreak did the noise begin to die down. We waited in the dugout until noon, wondering what had happened.

Had the attack succeeded? Were the Germans in retreat? Then Lieutenant Jackson appeared in the opening of the dugout.

"Right, men," he announced. "The attack has moved our position forward. This is where we come in. We have to run cables into what were the German bunkers so that we can keep our forward communication lines open, and we have to do it today, not tomorrow."

Charlie and I exchanged grins at this "we", which meant us poor ordinary soldiers. I'd never seen Lieutenant Jackson even hold a pick or a shovel except to hand it to one of us.

That afternoon we moved forward, laden down with rolls of cable and our picks and shovels. And, of course, our gas masks, just in case the Germans should launch a gas attack.

By mid-afternoon we were in what had been the German front-line trenches, running cables and setting up communication posts so that the officers at the Front could keep in touch with Base HQ. All along the trenches were dead German soldiers. Many of them were buried in mud-slides, with just their legs sticking out, or a hand, but now and then I came upon an upturned face. It was an appalling sight. The trouble was, after this time out in the trenches, I was getting hardened to it. That's one thing about war: the first time you see a dead body you shiver and shudder and you feel a bit sick. It's a shock. You can see yourself in that dead body. That's how I might look, you think to yourself. The next time it's still a shock, but not so much of one. Then after that, it's just another dead body, and the more you see, the less they affect you.

What struck me about these dead Germans, though, was how young so many of them looked. So many of them were just boys of about fourteen or fifteen, some even younger. Then it struck me that me and so many of the others on our side only *felt* old. I was just seventeen. So was Rob. Some of our soldiers were only fourteen or fifteen. We were still just boys.

We chose to set up the forward communication posts in what had been German dugouts. It seemed like a good idea because it saved making new ones. What surprised me was how well the German dugouts had been made. Unlike ours, which were just holes shored up with timber, the German dugouts were proper pillboxes, hidey-holes set in the ground made of concrete, with thick walls facing towards the Allied front line and on the sides. The back wall, though, was just a thin layer of cement. In the first one we went into we could see where it had fallen down in parts.

"Not very well built at the back," sniffed Terry. "Looks like they needed some good Tommy builders to come in and finish the job properly."

"Don't be an idiot," scoffed Ginger. "That's clever, that is. The back wall's thin because if the Hun had to retreat, like they have done now, then they don't have to use a lot of fire-power to punch a hole in it from their new positions, do they."

Terry looked at the hole and he gave a wry smile of admiration.

"Thinking two steps ahead!" he said. "You've got to hand it to 'em. They're clever beggars, and no mistake."

"Clever they may be, but it's us poor beggars who've got to reinforce that wall now," sighed Ginger. "More work for us!"

We spent the next week working knee-deep in mud, and sometimes waist-deep. As we worked, we heard rifle shooting as the snipers from both sides took pot-shots at each other. Then, without explanation, the Germans suddenly went quiet.

"Looks like we're winning, mates," said Wally, after the week was up. "I reckon the Huns must be building up to surrendering. We'll all be home for Christmas after all."

It was too much to hope for. Early the next morning a barrage of heavy artillery fire rained down on us. Shells going off, mud flying everywhere, the whole of our world going mad.

The Germans were launching their counter-attack.

We knew there was only one thing we could do if we were to have even a remote chance of staying alive. Retreat. The Germans knew precisely where to drop their shells to hit our positions because we were in their very own old trenches. As we struggled to make our way back through the water and mud, carrying as much of our equipment as we could manage, we found ourselves caught up with infantry units doing exactly the same thing.

We dived into dugouts, waiting a few minutes before squelching and sploshing through thick clinging mud to the next one. And all the time the German shells rained down around us. We kept our heads down and hoped the flying shrapnel wouldn't tear us to bits.

By nightfall we'd only managed to withdraw about 500 yards. The six of us had squeezed into yet another dugout and we'd been taking cover there for nearly an hour, with no sign of any let-up in the German bombardment.

"I can't stand this," grunted Ginger. "I'm going out to see if there's any way we can cut through to the reserve trench using some of the bomb-craters."

With that Ginger stepped outside, and promptly sank up to his waist in the mud.

"Just going for a quick swim, mates!" he laughed.

As we all started to laugh along with him there came an earth-shattering explosion from where he had been standing that hurled mud and smoke at us and poured more mud down on us from the ceiling of the dugout.

None of us could see because of the thick oily smoke. By force of habit, almost as soon as I started coughing I grabbed my gas mask and pulled it on over my face. But this was no gas attack. This was just smoke from a shell that had landed directly outside the dugout.

I felt the mud walls and roof of the dugout starting to cave in, and I grabbed Charlie and Wally by their sleeves and hauled them towards the entrance, and we stumbled out into the trench. Peter and Terry followed. We were just in time. Behind us the entrance to the dugout just collapsed, the whole wall of mud dropping down. If we'd still been in there we'd have been dead, buried under tons of mud.

I began to search around for Ginger in the hope that he'd survived the blast, that he might be just lying beneath a thin layer of mud, or under water. But I discovered, with a horror that made me retch, the first pieces of him, lying charred and still smoking in the mud.

Danny, Alf, and now Ginger. All dead. And I'm ashamed to admit that the next thought that struck me was: thank God it wasn't me.

For the next month we didn't leave the trenches. We just stayed there, living on what rations came up to us, and waiting for the orders to go forward and run more cables if our next attack succeeded. But it never did. We didn't move forward. And neither did the Germans. It was stalemate again.

"We're going to just die here like this in the mud," said Charlie one day. "All this time and no one's going anywhere. Not us, nor the Germans. All we do is go backwards and forwards and lose more and more men. I don't know why they don't just call it off."

"Who?" asked Wally.

"The top nobs from both sides," said Charlie. "They might as well play conkers and see who wins for all the point of this."

All the time I wondered how Rob was doing. What was it like for him in the fighting at the Front? Was he even still alive? Finally, in the second week of October, our unit were told that we were being sent back down the line to the Reserve Camp at Poperinghe. After almost eight weeks of nothing but mud and death, we were being relieved.

As soon as we got back to camp I grabbed myself a bath and changed my clothes, and then I set off in search of Rob. I wondered if his unit were back here, or if they were still at the Front.

I hurried towards tents where the Lonsdales and the rest of their makeshift unit were based, and one of the first faces I saw was good old Jed Lowe. My heart gave a leap of joy. If Jed was here then it meant that so was Rob.

"Jed!" I called.

He waved and hurried over towards me.

"Billy!" he said, and his face cracked into a sort of twisted grin. "It's good to see you're still alive."

"They can't keep us Carlisle blokes from popping up," I said, smiling. "Knock us down and we bounce up again." I looked towards the tents. "Where's Rob?" I asked. "Is he around?"

The grin vanished from Jed's face.

"Rob's dead, Billy," said Jed. "They shot him."

Even though the fear that it might happen had been in my thoughts for weeks now, to actually hear it said out loud hit me like a hammer blow. I could feel tears well up in my eyes, but I did my best to blink them away. It wouldn't be good for me to be seen crying, it wasn't manly. But … Rob. Dead.

"Rotten Germans," I snarled, hoping the tremble in my voice wouldn't show.

Jed shook his head. "It weren't the Germans," he said.

"It were our own side. A firing squad. They tied him to a post and shot him."

I stared at Jed, stunned. Rob shot by a firing squad? This I couldn't believe! I must have misheard. It was impossible! But the heavy gloom in Jed's voice told me it wasn't.

"It were a terrible thing," he said. "Terrible. Oughtn't to have been allowed to happen."

"But ... why?" I stammered.

"He wouldn't go," said Jed. "Weren't his fault. He'd been over the top more times than anyone. You know what Rob was like, nothing scared him. Like the rest of us, he'd seen his mates next to him cut in half by shrapnel, or blown to bits, or cut down by the Huns' machine-guns. I guess he just couldn't take it any more. We come to this attack and this junior officer – jumped-up little worm he was – ordered us over the top. Well it was obvious it was suicide. The Germans 'ad cut down the previous waves of men who'd gone over. Just mowed 'em down with their machine-guns like harvesting wheat.

" 'I'm not going. Not this time,' said Rob. 'We're all going to get killed and there won't be one dead German at the end of it. It's stupid. I'm not going.' So the junior officer had him placed under arrest.

"They court-martialled him and sentenced him to be shot for desertion. Him and some other young kid, who was only fifteen. The men in the firing squad could hardly bear to look at them." Jed shook his head at the thought. " 'Tain't right. They was only kids, really."

I walked around for the next two days in a daze. Rob dead. And shot by a firing squad from our own side! It was sickening. For Rob to be branded a coward and a deserter was unforgivable. He had been the bravest person I'd ever known. To me, the real cowards were the people who hid right back behind the fighting and gave the orders and put the death sentence on blokes like Rob.

Charlie tried to get me to talk about it, but at first I was so full of grief and anger that I didn't even want to think about what had happened to Rob. When I did finally talk to him about it, all my anger spilt out.

"They had no right to shoot him!" I said. "If he thought that the attack was pointless, then it was. Rob was no coward."

"Course he wasn't," said Charlie. "But he was working class, that was his real crime. If he'd been one of the toffs, or even a bit upper class, he'd have just been sent home to convalesce, nice and neat and tidy. If their class gets it it's called shell shock. It's only cowardice if it's our lot."

"I'd watch that talk, Charlie," muttered Wally. "Else they'll be saying you're one of them Bolsheviks like they got in Russia."

"Not me," said Charlie. "If you ask me, the Australians have got the right way of it. You don't see any class in their ranks."

Charlie was right. Whereas we could be punished if we didn't salute an officer properly, the Aussie privates didn't even call their commanding officers "sir", but called them by their first names. Our own commanders were shocked by the way the Australians acted and did their best to keep us away from them in case we tried to copy them.

To keep us in line the British commanders made sure that any breach of the rules, even the slightest, was heavily punished. Jed had told me about one of his outfit who was on leave and he'd had too much to drink, and when he got back to his billet he started singing and woke up his Sergeant.

Next morning he was up for orders before the Major and was charged with being drunk on active service. He got the maximum punishment, 28 days First Field Punishment, which meant he had to parade in full pack and go up and down the road at the double, watched by the Military Police. It was hard going because he had a full pack, tin helmet, all his stuff. Then, every morning and every night, he was spread-eagled and strapped by his wrists and ankles to the big wheel of one of the large guns for an hour. His pay was stopped straight away. What was worse, so was the allowance his wife got. I heard that his wife went to the Headquarters in London and asked why she wasn't getting her money. "Your husband's got himself in trouble," they told her, and there wasn't anything she could do about it.

Public punishments like this were done to make sure that the rest of us stayed in line and didn't disobey orders, if we didn't want to suffer the same fate. But, like Charlie said, these punishments only happened to ordinary soldiers, not the officers.

At the end of our seven days' rest at the reserve camp we went back to the Front. Back to the trenches and the mud, where life could change to death in just a second. Just in the time it took a bullet or a piece of shrapnel to fly through the air. I still couldn't get what had happened to Rob out of my mind. That could have been me. If I'd stayed in the infantry instead of being sent to join the Royal Engineers, that could have been me refusing to go over the top one last time. It could have been me tied to that post and shot by my own mates. I said as much to Charlie on our last night at the camp, but Charlie just scowled and said, "No it couldn't. You're a survivor, Billy, like me. Just so long as the Huns don't shoot us or drop a bomb on us like they did poor Ginger, you and me'll get through this. Someone's got to."

Stalemate continued all through October, with neither side making much ground and staying stuck in their own trenches. Now and then there was an offensive which gained a few yards, and then a retreat where the few yards gained were lost again. And so were a few hundred more men.

Morale was going down on our side. We hoped it was going down among the Germans as well. At this rate none of us would be home for this Christmas, or the next one, or even the one after that.

The Top Brass back at Base HQ must have been aware of how low morale was sinking because we were told that a brigadier was coming out to see for himself how we were doing in the trenches at the Front.

"We're having fun," muttered Charlie sarcastically under his breath. "Better than Blackpool."

The next day the Brigadier arrived. He looked as if he'd just stepped out from his tailor's, with his clean uniform and his boots all shiny. His manner was very confident, very full of himself, as if this war was just a small inconvenience that was interfering with his time. The Brigadier had only been in our trench for about half an hour when suddenly the Germans launched a bombardment. It was as if they knew the Brigadier was visiting.

I flung myself against the wet wall of the trench, sinking into the muddy water and keeping my head down in the hope that my helmet would keep my head safe. There was an explosion, then mud and water poured down on us.

I looked round. The Brigadier had stayed on the duckboards and was just crouching down. There was no expression on his face whatsoever. He looked like a man lost in thought. Mud rained down on him and he just crouched there. More explosions were heard. The mud wall I was pressing into shook and I thought it was going to fall on me.

"I'd advise you to get into the wall, sir!" shouted a sergeant major at the Brigadier.

The Brigadier shook his head. "Can't ruin these boots, Sarn't Major." He shouted to make himself heard above the explosions. "If I'd known the Hun was going to do this I'd have worn my second-best pair."

There were more explosions and then the sound of whistling, and then shrapnel was flying across the top of the trench, broken sheets of metal, their edges sharp as knives. They sank into the mud above us. How none of us were killed, I don't know. A few pieces of shrapnel fell into the trench, hissing when the hot metal met the cold water, but luckily none of them hit us.

As soon as there was a break in the German bombardment, the Brigadier's aide-de-camp ushered him away, along the trench to somewhere a little safer to continue his inspection.

I heard later that further along the trench some men had been hit by shrapnel during the attack and been killed. One man had put his head above the top of the trench and a piece of shrapnel had taken his head clean off, helmet and all.

A few days after the Brigadier's visit word filtered down the line that another big assault was planned.

"Not again!" groaned Charlie. "Every time we do a Big Attack it ends up the same. We get 500 yards forward, then we come back, and things go on the same until the next Big Attack."

"They say this one's going to be different," said Terry. "Everything's being thrown at the Hun at the same time. Our boys, the Aussies, the Canadians, the French. Everybody going at once. They reckon we're going to take Passchendaele Ridge."

"I can't see the point," Charlie shrugged. "With all this shelling that's gone on, I bet there's nothing left of it. It'll just be another big hole in the ground."

"Yeah," chuckled Wally, "but it'll be our hole in the ground, not the Germans'. Ain't that what this war's about?"

We had confirmation of what Terry had heard the next day. We had a new sergeant, Sergeant Peters, and he assembled us in the mud outside our dugout.

"Right, men," he told us. "We're going to make a big advance and push the Hun right back to Germany where he belongs. It's going to be done with everything we've got: tanks, planes and men. The infantry are going over the top, but they'll be lost without us Engineers. Without us laying cable lines right under their noses, they won't know where they are or what's happening. They have to be able to keep in touch with Command at all times, is that clear?"

"Yes, Sarge," we responded.

"Right. For this offensive, you're being attached to specific units. Your job is to keep them in communication, whatever happens. Morgan. Stevens."

"Yes, sir!" Charlie and I said the same time.

"You're with 74th Brigade. Crow. Parks. You're with the 1st Battalion of the Hertfordshires." And so on down the list, as Sergeant Peters attached us to fighting units.

A sinking feeling came into my stomach. This was it. After all our time in the reserve trenches, now we were being pushed forward for this major assault. We were going over the top. This should have been my moment of glory, the one I'd dreamed about when I was back in Carlisle, but now, with all I'd seen of this war, so many dead and just stalemate after stalemate, it didn't seem so glorious after all.

0500 hours on 12 October found me and Charlie, each loaded down with rolls of cable and our tools, crouched in the darkness in a trench along with the men from the 74th Brigade of Guards.

Each Guardsman had his rifle ready, bayonet fixed. The Lieutenant in charge seemed a decent sort of bloke. He was young, but he didn't throw his weight about. He spoke quietly and his air of confidence passed around our group.

The rum ration appeared and was passed along the line, each man taking a swig.

"Deadens the pain if you get hit," winked one Guardsman to me.

"Only if you drink a whole bottle," cracked another.

At 0515 hours our big guns opened up, pouring shells down on the German lines just yards away from us.

The Germans retaliated with their own barrage, and soon the early-morning sky above our heads was filled with tracers of fire, and the earth both behind and ahead of us rocked with the sounds of explosions. Mud hurled up and came down on top of us in showers.

The Lieutenant came over to Charlie and me. "There's a German pillbox about a hundred yards ahead," he told us. "You Engineers come over with the third wave. We should have cleaned the pillbox out by the time you get there. That's where I want you to set up the first communication point."

"Right, sir," I said.

The Lieutenant headed back down the line, checking his watch.

0520. 0525. As the hands of my watch moved to 0530, we saw the Lieutenant put his whistle to his lips … and then he blew, the shrill blast barely heard beneath the sounds of the artillery barrage, but the movement of the soldiers around us told us it was time. The attack was on.

The first wave of Guards went up the scaling ladders and over the top, crouching low, firing their rifles as they went. I noticed that the Lieutenant had been the first one over. The second wave soon followed. I could hear the chatter chatter chatter of machine-guns from the German lines, and the sound of our boys' rifles.

"OK, third wave!" said a voice.

Charlie and I looked at each other, then shook hands.

"Good luck, mate," said Charlie.

With that I grabbed the slippery rungs of the scaling ladder, and climbed up to the top of the trench, weighed down by the length of cable trailing behind me. This was surely hell on earth. Thick smoke hung over the mud. Dead and dying men were sprawled on the ground, some half in the mud, and the red lines of tracer fire kept coming. The distance we had to cover looked vast, even though it was only 100 yards or so. Already, many of the soldiers I had talked with in the trench lay on the ground, dead or dying.

"Come on!" yelled Charlie, and he began to run.

I joined him, moving as fast as I could with the mud dragging at my boots. Bullets smacked into the mud around me. It's amazing how fast you can move when your life is at stake. Now and then I felt myself stepping on a dead body and a couple of times I nearly lost my balance in the mud, but I put my head down, gritted my teeth and kept going.

As the Germans kept up their fire from their defensive positions I saw more soldiers around me stumble and then go down.

I neared the German lines and, through the smoke, saw the pillbox the Lieutenant had told us about, a concrete structure just visible sticking up from the mud. As I watched, one of our soldiers lobbed a grenade into the pillbox through one of the narrow openings, and then ducked away. There was the sound of a muffled explosion, and then smoke poured out from it, followed by the sound of screams as the Germans in the pillbox took the blast of the grenade. Then a couple of our soldiers dropped down into the German trench and I heard the sound of rifle fire.

Charlie and I reached the German trench and threw ourselves down into it. We were just in time. The spot where I'd been standing a second before erupted into a mass of flying wet clay as a German machine-gun poured its bullets into it.

Charlie and I dropped our rolls of cable and stood there, panting hard, trying to get our breath.

"Hurry up and get that line connected!" the Lieutenant shouted, then he charged forward, firing his pistol towards the German lines.

Charlie and I hurried inside the concrete pillbox. The three German soldiers inside were dead, their bodies lying twisted, their eyes still open.

"Better get them out first," I shouted.

We dragged the dead German soldiers out, and then set to work, hauling the cable in and setting up a telegraph point inside the pillbox. The Guards had moved on and were already attacking the next line of German defence, but the sound of rifle fire was so close we could tell that they were meeting very stiff opposition.

The Lieutenant appeared in the entrance to the pillbox just as we finished making the connections to the wire. "Are we in contact yet?" he demanded.

"Nearly, sir," said Charlie. "Just a minute more."

"Good man," said the Lieutenant. And with that he went out again to see how the forward troops were getting on.

In fact, that 100 yards was as far as we managed to advance that day. Or the next, come to that. The Germans poured everything they had down on to us, heavy shells, machine-guns, tracers, gas, but we just bunkered down and stayed where we were.

Charlie and I took it in turns to operate the telegraph-receiving key, while the other secured the line. On my stint at the key I started to get reports through from the other divisions on how they'd fared in the Big Attack, and I learnt that the Guards Division that Charlie and I were with had done well to get this far. Other units hadn't done so well. The main assault on what remained of the village of Poelcapelle on the Passchendaele Ridge by a joint force of British and Australians had been a disaster. The 2nd Australian and the British 49th and 66th Divisions had been all but wiped out in the attack.

The same story was repeated all along the line. Unit after unit had been wiped out, and only about 100 yards of ground gained in a few places, like ours.

Reports also came in about our tank offensives. Those great lumbering heavy machines had been unleashed, intended to force their way through the wire and right through the German lines. But tank after tank had got stuck in the mud, sinking so deep that their tracks couldn't haul them out. Bogged down like that, they'd been sitting targets for the German heavy guns.

It looked like the attempt to take Passchendaele had stalled.

The next day, the Germans launched a counter-offensive against our position. The machine-guns along our new trench top kept up a steady stream of fire, a constant barrage of noise that made it difficult for me to listen to the messages coming through the wires properly. All the time the German artillery kept up their attack on our positions – and still the rain came down.

## NOVEMBER–DECEMBER 1917

During the weeks that followed, we maintained our front-line position. The attacks from both sides kept on and the rain kept coming down. Men died and lay where they fell, or were wounded and were stretchered back to the dressing camps. The badly wounded got a "Blighty Ticket", which meant they would be sent back home.

Whatever High Command said about this war being over by Christmas and the Germans being defeated, in our trenches our belief that this war would ever be over began to fade.

And then, on 6 November, the news came over the telegraph wires that the Canadians had broken through the German lines and taken Passchendaele itself. The Germans were in retreat! The War was over!

Over the next week, I listened as the reports came in over the wires. The Canadian Corps had been the victors at Passchendaele, but had lost 16,500 men in the battle. Elsewhere along the line, our forces had pushed forward. There was now a new front line, just a few hundred yards further forward from the old front line. The Germans had moved back, but they were still there, just 100 yards or so away from our lines. The War was far from over – we were back at stalemate.

December finally came. The rain poured down as heavy as ever. The heavy guns kept up their barrage on both sides. The shooting from rifles and machine-guns continued from every infantry trench.

And then, one morning as dawn was coming up, Charlie and I came out of our pillbox and just stood there, listening, unable to believe our ears.

Silence.

Nothing. Not from our guns, nor the German guns. Not from any guns anywhere along the lines. Everything was quiet and still. It had even stopped raining at last!

"Maybe the War's over," I whispered, afraid to speak too loudly in case I disturbed the silence.

"No," said Charlie, also whispering, in awe at the stillness. "Do you know what day it is? It's Christmas Day."

We looked at one another as it sunk in. Charlie was right. Christmas Day.

"Happy Christmas," said Charlie. Then he looked around us, at the trench, the mud, and laughed. "We'd better get our Christmas dinner prepared," he grinned. "What'll it be? Roast turkey? Duck? Chicken? Christmas pud with custard?"

"No," I chuckled. "Let's have something really special today. Let's have tinned bully beef and biscuits."

And we both laughed.

A call from further along the trenches caught our attention. It was a Guardsman from the forward front trench.

"Hey, lads!" he called. "You should come along and hear what's happening up the Front!"

Intrigued, Charlie and me splashed our way through the mud along the reserve trench, and then made our way through the communication trench to the front line.

Some soldiers had climbed to the top and their heads were above the top of the trench, and they were straining their ears to listen to something. In the eerie silence, we could hear voices calling to us from the German trenches, drifting across the mud and barbed wire of No Man's Land.

"Hey, Tommy!" called a German voice. "Happy Christmas!"

The soldier at the top of the ladder nearest to us looked down at us, grinned, and said in surprise, "What d'you know? They're sending us Christmas greetings!"

"Well don't be a sourpuss, Jim!" said another soldier. "Send 'em back."

"Right," said Jim. He hauled himself higher up the ladder.

"Careful," warned another of the soldiers. "It might be a trick. Stick your head too far over the top and they might shoot it off."

"If they do you can stick some holly in it and put it on the table like a Christmas pudding," joked Jim. Then he called towards the German lines: "Hey, Fritz! Can you hear me?"

There was a pause, then the German soldier shouted back: "I hear you, Tommy!"

"Good!" shouted Jim. "Merry Christmas from all of us here!"

There was a pause, and then we heard more voices calling from the German lines: "Merry Christmas to you!"

"Ask 'em what they're having for Christmas dinner," said another soldier.

"You ask 'em, Jack," said Jim. "I don't see why I should be doing all the shouting."

Jack climbed up another of the scaling ladders until he, too, had his head well above the top of the trench.

"Hey, Fritz!" he called. "What are you having for Christmas dinner?"

"We are having rat!" called back the German.

"Rat?" echoed Jack. "Is that all?"

"*Ja*, Tommy," came the German's reply. "But it is a very big fat rat. Lots of meat on it! What are you having?"

"Oh, the usual!" called Jack. "Roast beef. Roast potatoes. Gravy. Brussels sprouts." Then he laughed and added, "That's providing my butler gets here with it in time in my car!"

All us lads in the trench laughed, and we heard the Germans laugh too.

Suddenly we heard the noise of something coming through the air towards us from the German trenches.

"They're chucking something!" called Jim.

"Grenades!" yelled one soldier, and we all ducked.

Instead, something hit the top of the trench and lay there. Jack picked it up and showed it to us.

It was a small rock. Tied to it was a packet of German cigarettes.

"Happy Christmas, Tommy!" called the voice. "A present from us to you!"

We watched as Jack untied the packet of cigarettes. He took one, and then passed the packet down. "Here you are mates," he said. "A Christmas present from Kaiser Bill's men. Pass them around."

"We got to give them something back," said Charlie. "We can't just take them and leave it like that."

"You're right," I agreed. "But what?"

"I'm not giving them my tobacco," said one soldier firmly.

"Me, neither," said another.

There was much nodding of heads at this in general agreement.

"Come on, mates, we don't want to be seen to be mean," said Jim.

"How about chucking over a tin of bully beef?" suggested another soldier.

"What, and poison 'em for Christmas?" I said, and the others laughed.

"I've got a flask with some rum in it," said one soldier. "I've been saving up my rations. It's only a little flask."

"Sounds good to me," said Jack. "OK, Shorty, hand it up and I'll chuck it over."

Shorty rummaged around in his kit and produced a battered metal flask. He handed it up the ladder to Jack. "Here you are," he said. "But make sure you throw it right the way over. I don't want it ending up in the middle of No Man's Land and going to waste."

Jack held the flask in his hand, and then looked towards the German lines. I saw the look of doubt on his face. "I don't know," he said. "Throwing a rock is one thing. It's hard to judge the weight of this, with the rum sloshing around inside it like that."

"I'll throw it," I offered.

Charlie gave me a doubtful look. "You reckon you can get it over there?" he asked.

"If a Hun can throw a rock, I can throw that the same distance," I said.

Jack came down the ladder and handed me the metal flask.

"OK," he said. "Over to you."

I climbed up the ladder. Although there was still no shooting, I couldn't stop myself from hesitating before I put my head over the top of the trench, it had become such a force of habit.

Then I hauled myself over the top and stood there, looking out over the expanse of clayey, potholed, bomb-shelled ground, strewn with barbed wire. Everyone and everything else was below ground level.

I looked towards the German lines. "Where are you, Fritz?" I called. "We've got a Christmas present for you!"

A head with a German helmet poked up from behind the lines, about 70 yards away. "Here, Tommy!" he called. And he waved his arm.

I held the flask in my hand and measured the distance to the German lines in my mind.

I pulled my arm back, crouched, and then shouted: "Merry Christmas, Fritz! Have a drink on us!"

And then I let fly, swinging my arm round as hard as I could and putting as much force as I could into my throw.

The metal flask sailed up into the air, glinting as it caught the light from the sun's early rays. Then it came down … down … and disappeared into the German trench.

We heard a loud cheer go up from the German lines, and then the German's head popped back into view again. He was holding the flask and he waved it at me.

"Thank you, Tommy!" he shouted. "We will drink your health today!"

I clambered down the ladder from the top of the trench, and the soldiers in the trench grinned broadly at me and clapped.

"With a throw like that, you ought to be playing cricket for England, lad," said Jim.

Just then a young lieutenant appeared from the reserve trench, accompanied by a sergeant. "What's all this noise going on!" he demanded.

"Just exchanging Christmas presents with Fritz, sir!" said Jack. "A packet of cigs for a flask of rum."

The Lieutenant didn't seem impressed.

He looked along the line at each of us, unsmiling, and then he said in clipped tones: "Fraternizing with the enemy is an offence liable to court martial. I'd stop it if you don't want to find yourself in serious trouble. Don't forget, tomorrow you'll be killing them again. And they'll be killing you."

With that he turned and headed back to the reserve trench. The Sergeant gave us a look that seemed to say "Sorry, blokes, nothing I can do about it." Then the Sergeant went after the Lieutenant.

Shorty looked down at the packet of German cigarettes that were now in his hand. There was one left in the packet. He took it out and put it to his lips.

"It's a present and it's Christmas," he said. "It's more than I got from any general in this army, so I'm keeping it."

And then, strangest of all, we heard the sound of singing coming from the German trenches.

"It's a carol," said Charlie. "They're singing 'Silent Night' in German."

It seemed so strange, being here in this place surrounded by so much death and destruction and misery, and hearing that beautiful sound carrying on the air, a song I'd known and sung ever since I was a child. I remembered Rob and me singing it when we were at junior school, every Christmas. I couldn't help it, but I found myself singing along with them, but in English. And Charlie joined in, and then Jack, and then we were all of us singing, English voices and German voices mixed together singing the same tune.

If I live to be a hundred, I'll never forget that special Christmas Day. No presents, no special dinner, nothing but men on opposing sides in a war joining together to sing just one carol.

Then it was over.

The rest of that day was strange. Still no bombs, no shooting, just me and my mates being kind of quiet together and thinking about our families back home. We wondered how they were, and if they were thinking of us out here. It struck me that I hadn't written a letter home for ages, not since I'd been at Base HQ. Mum would kill me when I got back home for not writing.

At midnight exactly, the big guns started up again, from both sides. Christmas was over. It was just as the Lieutenant had said: once again, we were killing them, and they were killing us. Four years on, and we were still at war.

## Epilogue
## January 1918 – June 1919

My war ended on 6 January 1918 just outside Passchendaele. I was hit by a German shell. Once again, I was lucky to be alive, but this time my left arm and left leg were smashed by shrapnel. At the Casualty Station they talked about amputating both my leg and my arm, but again I was lucky: the doctor who treated me insisted that he could reset them enough so that they would mend. I would always walk with a limp, and it would take time before I could use my left arm again, but at least I wouldn't lose them.

I was sent back home to England. First I went to a military hospital on the northern outskirts of London at a place called Mill Hill. There I wrote home to Mum and Dad and told them what had happened and that I was alive, and I'd be returning home as soon as I was able.

I also wrote the hardest letter I've ever had to write. This one was to Mrs Matthews, Rob's mum, telling her how sorry I was about what had happened to him, and not to believe the worst of him. I told her how Rob was the bravest soldier I'd known all the time I was out there, and that what had happened to him was wrong. She wrote back. It was just a short letter, but she never had been very good at reading and writing. It meant a lot to me that she managed to write back.

I went back home to Carlisle in June. I was able to walk, even though I used a stick to help me get about. I thought my mum would be angry when she saw me again and say "I told you so!" when she saw me with my stick, but when I knocked at our door and she opened it, she threw her arms around me and burst into tears.

By September of 1918 everyone reckoned the War was as good as over. The Germans were in retreat on all fronts and our side was pushing forward all the time. The end came in November 1918 when the Germans finally surrendered.

In June 1919, they put up a monument in Carlisle with the names of the local men who'd gone out to the War and died. The name of Robert Matthews wasn't on it. I went along to see the local Council with Mrs Matthews and asked that they put Rob's name on it, but this little official with a small moustache said to us: "We don't put the names of cowards on the same memorial as brave men." I got angry then and asked him which part of the War he'd fought in, knowing full well he'd stayed safely back in Carlisle the whole time, but Mrs Matthews asked me not to make a fuss, so I shut up and took her back home. But it didn't stop me feeling angry.

I still feel angry every time I pass that memorial, and one day, I swear, I'm going to make sure that Rob's name gets carved on that memorial. He deserves to be there, along with all the others who died out there in the mud of Flanders.

# HISTORICAL NOTE

The roots of the First World War, which lasted from 1914 until 1918, can be traced back to the Franco-Prussian War of 1870–1871. During this war, France was defeated by Germany, and France's eastern provinces, Alsace and Lorraine, became part of a new and larger unified Germany. From that moment, Germany seemed determined to continue to expand and become the leading world power. Aware of Germany's intentions, other European nations – including Britain and Russia – began to prepare for war. For its part, France was determined to get Alsace-Lorraine back from Germany. Germany was aware of this, and also aware that it might also have to fight a war against the Russians who were military allies of France. The German strategy, developed by Count Alfred von Schlieffen in 1905, was that if war was declared, Germany would attack and defeat France first and then attack Russia.

The spark that ignited the War was the assassination of Archduke Franz Ferdinand of Austria and his wife in Sarajevo on 28 June 1914. As a result, Austria-Hungary declared war on Serbia. Two days later Czar Nicholas II put his Russian army in support of Serbia. Germany, acting in support of her ally, Austria-Hungary, demanded that Russia stand down. Russia refused and Germany declared war on Russia.

Putting the von Schlieffen strategy into action, on August 2 Germany demanded from neutral Belgium the right of passage through its land to attack France. Belgium refused, and on August 4, German troops invaded Belgium.

Britain was bound by a treaty to guarantee Belgium's safety if Belgium was ever attacked. Britain was also aware that if the Channel ports fell to an enemy, then Britain was at risk from invasion. So on 4 August 1914 at 11pm (London time), Britain declared war on Germany.

The reason it became a World War rather than just a European War was because all the major European powers, including Britain, Germany and France, were Empires with colonies overseas. Britain's colonies spread as far as Australia and New Zealand, Canada and India. All these colonies then joined the War in support of their "home" country. So, for example, soldiers from British units stationed in Africa were in conflict with soldiers from German units also stationed there, and so fighting broke out between them, although not with the same intensity as in Europe. Many of the British colonies also sent troops to Europe to fight in the War.

More alliances were formed as other countries across

the world took sides and got drawn into the War. In 1917 America, which had so far been neutral, entered the War on the side of the two main Allies, Britain and France, although the main body of their troops did not arrive in Europe until 1918.

It was on the Western Front, in the fields of Flanders in Belgium that most of the casualties occurred. The casualty figures for the battlefield conflict alone were:

**France:** 1,385,300 dead, 3,614,700 wounded
**Germany:** 1,808,545 dead, 4,247,143 wounded
**British Empire:** 947,023 dead, 2,313,558 wounded
**USA:** 115,660 dead, 210,216 wounded

**Total:** 4,256, 528 dead and 10,385,617 wounded
– making 14,642,145 casualties in all

To put this into perspective (from the British side): it meant that 12 per cent of the total number of British soldiers who served on the Western Front were killed (that's one soldier in every eight), while nearly 38 per cent were wounded. In other words, half of all the British soldiers who went to France became casualties of the war.

The muddy quagmires that were the battlefields of the Western Front, which themselves contributed so much to the deaths of so many, were the result of the heavy shells used by both sides. The fields of Flanders lay on non-absorbent clay, and over generations a network of drains had been constructed just beneath the surface of the fields, to drain rainwater from the fields into the sea. The bombing smashed these drains. With the water unable to escape, the fields soon turned to mud.

During the years of war on the Western Front the front line swung backwards and forwards from time to time, but there was little decisive change. Sometimes the Germans would make advances, and sometimes the Allies – with often just a few hundreds yards being gained by each side. The stalemate between both sides on the Western Front, which included the battle at Passchendaele, continued until August 1918 when the Allies made a major break-through of the German lines at Amiens. From that moment the German military machine began to crumble. During August and September, major advances by the Allies pushed the German forces further back. By October 1918 the German leaders were sending out peace-notes to the Western leaders.

The War finally ended on 11th November 1918. On that day the Armistice was signed. Two days before this it had been announced that the German Kaiser, Wilhelm II, had abdicated and had gone into exile, and a German Republic had been proclaimed.

The First World War was over.

However, for one German soldier who served in the trenches on the Somme, it was just the beginning. A British shell had hit the trench and killed most of the German soldiers in it. This particular soldier was lucky and he escaped with just minor injuries. His name was Adolf Hitler.

## Christmas truces on the Western Front

On the first Christmas Day of the War, 25 December 1914, there was an unofficial truce between the ordinary German and British troops in the opposing trenches. They came out of their trenches and met in No Man's Land, where they shook hands, wished one another a Happy Christmas, and exchanged souvenirs. Some even posed for photographs together.

Perhaps the most famous event of this 1914 Christmas truce was the football game between British soldiers and German soldiers played in No Man's Land.

After this truce of 1914, there were no further examples of such close fraternization between the men of both sides, although the other Christmas Days right up to the end of the war in 1918 were marked by a ceasefire by both sides, and an exchange of shouted greetings, and an occasional exchange of small gifts such as cigarettes.

## TIMELINE

**June 1914** Assassination of Archduke Franz Ferdinand at Sarajevo. Austria attacks Serbia.

**July 1914** Austria and Hungary at war with Russia.

**August 1914** Germany declares war on Russia and France and invades Belgium. Great Britain declares war on Germany.

**September 1914** First trenches of the Western Front are dug.

**December 1914** Unofficial Christmas truce declared by Western Front soldiers.

**April 1915** Battles of Aisne and Ypres.

**September 1915** Battle of Loos. Italy joins War on side of Allies. Austro-German invasion of Poland.

**February 1916** The longest battle of the War, Verdun, begins. Neither side wins, but there are an estimated one million casualties.

**July–November 1916** Battle of the Somme – about a million casualties, but little ground gained by Allies.

**December 1916** David Lloyd George is elected Prime Minister of Great Britain. Battle of Verdun ends.

**March 1917** Tsar Nicholas II of Russia abdicates. Germany launches first of five major offensives to try and win the war.

**April 1917** USA declares war on Germany. Mutinies in French army begin.

**June 1917** Battle of Messines – British explode nineteen mines under the ridge.

**October 1917** Battle of Passchendaele. Russian workers revolt against the ruling classes – leads to Armistice between Russia and Germany.

**March 1918** Treaty of Brest-Litovsk ends Russian participation in the War.

**July 1918** Former Russian Tsar, Nicholas II and his family murdered by Bolshevik rebels.

**August–September 1918** Allied offensive on Western Front forces German retreat.

**November 1918** Allied-German armistice. German naval fleet surrenders. Kaiser Wilhelm II of Germany abdicates. Germany proclaimed a Republic.

**June 1919** Treaty of Versailles signed between Allies and Germany.

**July 1919** Cenotaph unveiled in London to commemorate the dead.

# PICTURE ACKNOWLEDGEMENTS

New recruits – many young men lied about their age in order to join the British army.

New recruits in training in 1914.

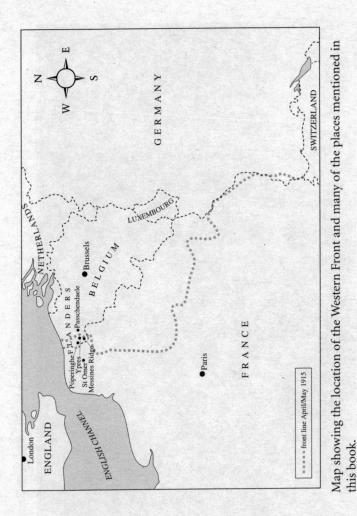

Map showing the location of the Western Front and many of the places mentioned in this book.

A British soldier emerging from a dugout in a trench.

Sir Douglas Haig, Commander-in-chief of the British Forces in France and Flanders.

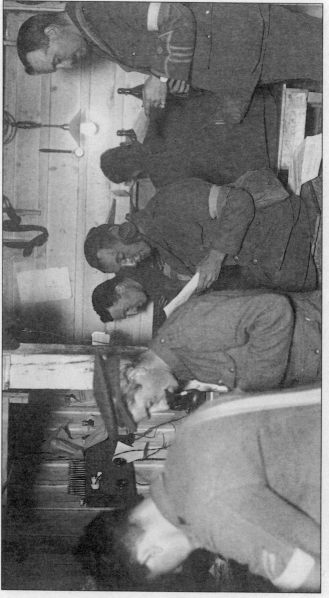

Royal Engineers at work in a captured German dugout in September 1916.

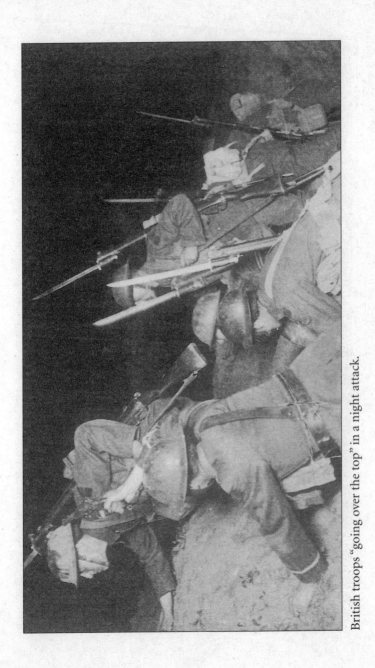

British troops "going over the top" in a night attack.

A soldier speaks on the telephone in the field. Telegraph wires allowed regiments to communicate with headquarters.

British and German soldiers pictured during the unofficial Christmas truce in January 1915.